Big Red's Daughter

Black Curtain Press
PO Box 632
Floyd VA 24091

ISBN 13: 978-1627551038

First Edition
10 9 8 7 6 5 4 3 2 1

Big Red's Daughter

John McPartland

Chapter One

He was driving an MG—a low English-built sports car— and he was a tire-squeaker, the way a wrong kind of guy is apt to be in a sports car. I heard the squeal of his tires as he gunned it, and then I saw him cutting in front of me like a red bug. My car piled into his and the bug turned over, spilling him and the girl with him out onto the street.

By the time our iron touched I'd swung my car to the right, so it wasn't much of a crash. I climbed out in a hurry, angry and ready to go.

The MG pilot was up and ready to go, too. The girl was beside him, brushing the skirt over her long legs. Nobody drew even a scratch out of the bump.

This was a tall, lean lad with a pale face and hot, dark eyes. I saw that much before his left fist smashed into my face. Not a Sunday punch—a real fighter's hard, straight left.

I was looking up at the cloud-rimmed blue sky. My face was numb; this boy had a solid, exploding punch. I tried to roll over fast—stomping on the down man's face is popular these days. I was right but I was slow. I saw the heel coming down and I brought my hands up. But the heel swung back from me and I pushed up into a low crouch.

The girl had him from behind, pulling his jacket down over his wide shoulders, her right knee high in the small of his back. This was a girl who must have seen action. She knew just the trick to keep her boy friend from grinding my nose into my teeth with his heel.

I was up and ready again, but he was satisfied with his one-punch job. He was laughing, his head back, his narrow face white, his teeth gleaming in the sunlight.

The girl had been talking to him, slow and low, and he nodded, turned his head, and smiled at her. Real tall boy, maybe six-four, slim, maybe one-eighty. She was tall for a girl, bronze-blonde hair cut short, and she looked smooth and fine, even now.

A dozen or so people were standing around us now and more were running up.

"I got a little hot," the tall boy said to me. "We'll go into it later. Let's get the stuff out of the street." The girl put her knee down and let go of his coat. He was smiling at me, but his black eyes were watching for the first flicker of a muscle in my arms and shoulders.

"We'll go into it later," I agreed, and our eyes met. Neither of us would look away. All I could see now were those black eyes of his, and I guess all he could see were mine, which are a kind of gray, I think.

Another ten seconds of staring and we'd have gone at it again. I was willing, breathing hard but with a loose, balanced readiness for him this time. A boy with a left like a rifle shot and the kind that finished you off when he had you down... It would be interesting.

There was a mumble of talk around us and then the law came through the crowd. This was the fancy little town of Carmel-by-the-Sea in California, and the law is professional and competent, the way the law usually is when there are lots of millions of dollars around.

He looked away first when we heard the policeman's voice. I knew two things about the tall, lean, pale-faced boy now. He was a mean, solid fighter. He'd looked away first.

Three things. He was a show-off in a sports car.

And I knew another thing about him. He was with a fine, beautiful girl who had sleek, golden legs and some tricks of her own. Since I knew I was going to try him out again, I figured I might as well know her, too.

The watching citizens, the boy, the law, and I pushed the MG right side up again. It was a little crumpled on the side, nothing else. The girl was dusting herself off now, and I looked at her for a couple of moments before going back to my own car. The left fender was bent in against the front tire. I pulled it out.

By now there was a police car and the crowd was a lot of intent faces that watched the tall lad, the girl, and me as if we were a trained-dog act. The law was friendly. There was no real damage and nobody was hurt, so they took our names and statements and called it a day.

Her name was Wild Kearny. Not a nickname or something

coy that a press agent dreamed up—that really was her name, Wild, after her mother's people, she explained to the officer. She lived in Carmel but home was back East, Connecticut.

The slim boy with the hard fists was a simple Robert Brown up from Los Angeles. Wild called him Buddy when she spoke to him, and that turned out to be what everybody called him —Buddy Brown.

I gave my name and the rest of it to the soft-voiced man in the uniform. Jim Work. Twenty-five. Home was Chicago. On the Monterey Peninsula to go to school. Three weeks out of the Army. Yeah, I'd been to Korea. No, I didn't think much of Korea. The officer turned out to have been there too. He didn't think much of it either.

Everybody was being nice to each other now, so the crowd drifted off. The law checked our drivers' licenses and the stuff on the steering posts, gave us that last up-and-down look, and then climbed back into the patrol car.

The three of us were comparatively alone now in the bright sunlight of a Saturday afternoon in January on the golden coast of California.

"Well, boy?" said Buddy Brown. He was smiling, as if he remembered the last time he'd been in something like this, and how much trouble there'd been, and how much fun it was.

"You don't drive an MG for sour bat splat," I said.

"Let's go somewhere and you show me how I should drive my car," Buddy said, and now his mouth had an eager twist.

"We'll go to the Zoo," said Wild Kearny.

I was going to have to take this Buddy Brown. Because Wild Kearny looked like the kind of girl that would be with winners, not losers, top winners in the top tournaments and never the second-flight or the almost-good-enough. Not the kind of girl that I'd ever known.

"You want to go to the Zoo and see the people, boy?" asked Buddy.

"Any place, any time," I said.

"Latch on." They slid into the buckets of the MG and Wild waved at me.

I got into my car. Buddy squeaked his tires and headed down the street. I followed.

It had been three weeks since the lieutenant at Fort Ord, a

dozen miles away, had given me the few hundred dollars I had coming and the certificate that said I'd put in twenty-three months for my uncle. There was nobody back in Chicago except some of my dad's people, no job with any beat to it, no real reason for going back.

The Monterey Peninsula had a nice little college, some of the best bars I'd ever seen, a lot of action, three fine golf courses, and blue skies in January. You're twenty-five for only one year, so it might as well be a good year. I was going to use it up in the best part of the country I'd seen yet—around Monterey.

The red MG clipped around a corner and scuttled up a narrow, tree-wrapped road. I followed some twenty yards behind. This part of Carmel I liked fine—lots of trees, plenty of flowers, comfortable little houses nearly hidden away. Downtown Carmel was set up to make tourists say quaint, but up here in the hills it looked like good living.

Anyway, January in Chicago was never like this. Or Korea.

Buddy Brown whipped the MG into a short driveway and stopped, pulled up behind him and watched Wild Kearny get out. She was one beautiful girl. Her body was graceful without effort. Her hair was a tiger gold, natural and lovely, her face was that of somebody's pretty young sister grown up to be a woman.

The slim, tall lad uncoiled his long legs, slipped out from behind the wheel, and stood looking at me.

"What happens now?" I asked, walking up to him. Wild stood there, cool, indifferent eyes on me. I was the stranger who'd bumped Buddy's car and then had been knocked flat in a one-punch fight. The stranger whose nose, teeth, and face bones she'd saved from being hash. Just some guy.

To me Wild Kearny was the one girl. A couple of minutes watching her and I knew that. She had the beauty, the fire, the elegance that only one girl could have for me.

"Nothing happens now," she said. "We go in and listen to some music. That's all. Another girl and I live here. We call it the Zoo. A cageless zoo."

There were two other cars parked next to the little house, a gray foreign car and a low, shiny-black two-seater Jaguar. My '49 Ford was an awkward elephant beside them.

They went ahead and I looked at the gray beauty. It was a

Nash-Healey; I'd read about them, but I'd never seen one before. Jaguars and MG's were common around the Peninsula, but this Healey was new to me.

Wild's house was a board-and-bat cottage, weathered a soft gray, with lots of vines and flowers almost covering it. I followed her and Buddy down three stone steps into a sizable room with a fireplace. A girl and three young men looked up at us, and the girl waved a hand at Wild, then eyed me with mild interest. The girl was pretty without Wild's blood-heating beauty.

Wild passed names around casually. The girl was Pen Brooks. She smiled, checked my clothes, my build, and some intangibles that girls seem to know about, and looked away.

I don't remember the names of the men. One of them wore wrinkled cotton slacks and a turtle-neck sweater; one was in charcoal flannels; the third had on a gabardine shirt, jodhpurs, and boots. They were the crew-cut Princeton type. I knew what anyone would know about these three: They'd have money and know how to spend it, they'd have women, and they'd live in the casually expensive way most people only read about.

Buddy was watching me, and our eyes met. We sure didn't like each other, but he was one up on me. He could laugh at me.

Wild went into the kitchen, up a couple of steps from the living room, and came back with three tall glasses of beer. The other four went back to listening to the Stan Kenton record, not new, and not saying much. There were some golf clubs in a leather job on the floor, and on a bookcase was a Rolleiflex with a flash gun. The record player was high-fidelity, and the whole place had an easy air of the best being just good enough.

"You like Kenton?" Buddy asked, smiling.

"He's changed a lot," I answered. "Now he's saying something, or trying to say something, that I don't quite understand. Maybe he doesn't, either, but he's trying to say it anyway."

Wild was looking at us, listening. Buddy nodded. "That's very good, boy."

"Always the rat, Buddy," Wild said, standing up. She turned to me. "I liked what you said about Kenton." She knew she had me—a girl can sense that awfully fast—and I think she was a little embarrassed and maybe a little sorry for me.

"How about Dave Brubeck? What's he saying?" Buddy

asked.

"I've heard him only a couple of times. I don't know."

"What are you going to do about my car?" The change of pace was intentional. His face didn't change at all. Now he was waiting for me to protest, to say he'd cut in front of me, to get off balance. Wild had been friendly to me and I knew that made him angry. To Buddy there was only one stage and the only person in the spotlight was him, and there were only women in the audience. Men were to fight and to whip, to be smashed.

"You got any insurance?" I asked.

"What's that got to do with it?"

"Maybe they'll pay."

"You broke? You don't have any money?"

None of the others bothered to watch or listen. I could feel Wild's eyes on me. I wondered how many men she had watched being pushed around by Buddy.

"You don't know how to drive. You're a punk," I said. I waited for that snake-striking left. It didn't come.

He looked quiet and thoughtful. "There's a little space in back. Maybe you want to take your shirt and jacket off first?" He was untying his bow tie now, unbuttoning his white nylon shirt.

The boy in the hound's-tooth vest looked up and shook his head. "Killer Brown is loose again."

"You'd think it would bore him. It bores everyone else," said Fen Brooks.

I stripped down to the waist, as Buddy was doing. He was lean, with unusually wide shoulders and more muscle than most thin men have. Wild drank her beer.

"Good luck, fellow," said the turtle-neck-sweater guy. "You have our very best hopes."

"Try not to be noisy." This was the boy in jodhpurs.

Brown and I went out in back. There was a cleared space of bare dirt. Brown kicked my ankle out from under me and hit me as I fell.

Chapter Two

He let me get up because he wanted to have fun. I was way off balance and he tagged me twice in the face, snapping my head back. He was trying to cut my lips against my teeth. I came back close in. This guy's long, rattlesnake arms would cut me bad if we stayed apart.

I got in close, all right; he lifted my head right up off my shoulders with the heel of his left hand coming up under my chin. This time while I was trying to get up, he kicked me in the head and the ribs a few times.

There was a sackful of pain and the sack was me.

Maybe he looked at me after he kicked me, maybe he just walked away. After some time I pulled myself into a sitting position.

There was no reason to curse Brown. He'd taken me. Tripping to start the fight was O.K. in his rulebook, a knife or a set of knucks would be O.K. in his rulebook, and I had to play his rules or get out of the game. I wasn't getting out of the game.

Pen Brooks and one of the boys came out and helped me up. Pen had a wet cloth and she washed my face a little. Not because she cared; I think she was curious to see what a beaten man looked like, and a little too stuffy just to come out and stare.

"You O.K., fellow? Can you make it home all right?" the man in the turtle-neck sweater was asking me.

"Yeah, sure," I mumbled.

"Buddy's certainly tough to beat." Pen was speaking to him, not to me. I could tell, because the tone was different.

The man didn't like it. "Yeah, he's a real tough guy."

Pen smiled. Her mouth was half open, her eyes were bright. She was excited, the way girls get. Not for me, though.

"Better have him come in the house for a minute or two. He looks like he's oozing around a little."

"He's kind of messy."

"That'll be all right. We can always clean up."

I felt stupid and clumsy. That hurt more than my face or

the aching weakness around my kidneys. The turtle-neck-sweater boy actually had to help me walk back into the house.

Wild Kearny was in a big chair, her long golden legs over one side, yellow skirt high over her knees. A George Shearing record was spinning in the player.

"I'm sorry," she said, looking up at me, "but this time you asked for it."

"I didn't do very good." It was hard to talk. My mouth was a little swollen and crusted.

"Go in there and wash up. Maybe a beer or something afterward." She looked away. The one girl in the world for me and her boy had just worked me over without even breathing hard. I turned and stared at Buddy Brown. He was standing by the fireplace and I could hear him talking to the man in the hounds-tooth vest.

"So these two Paris hipsters take the boat to America. They come into New York Harbor and they see the Statue of Liberty. One cat turns to the other and says, 'Dig that crazy Ronson!'"

The vest guy laughed. Brown looked across the room at me.

"Hello, punk," he said, and his face was quiet and serious. The laugh was inside.

I went to the bathroom and began to wash the dirt from my face and hands. One of the boys brought me my shirt and jacket. I put them on and looked at myself in the mirror. It's wonderful, I thought, to be twenty-five in a lazy town like Carmel and a sucker for a dirty fighter like Buddy Brown.

I went back to the big room. Wild Kearny was still in her chair, but Buddy Brown was gone. The others were sitting around drinking beer, talking a little, laughing, listening. This time it was an old Artie Shaw.

"Come over and sit down, if you want to," said Wild. "There's beer on the other side of that door."

A carton of cans of beer, cold with little trickles of dew, stood on the table beyond the door. I punctured a can and walked back to Wild. It hurt a little getting down to the floor beside her chair.

"Feel all right?" she asked.

"No good." The beer tasted fine, stinging a little on the cut in my lip.

"Buddy took off. He's going to try to find a shop open to

pound out the dents. He won't drive a car that's not wedding-night perfect."

"Wedding nights are perfect?" It was a strange phrase to use about a car, I thought.

"It says so," answered Wild. She had enormous, lovely eyes.

"What's 'it'?"

She laughed. "You know what 'it' is. 'It' is what makes all the rules and says how things have to be. Like wedding nights, for instance, the girls, and how to play doubles tennis, or what to drink at what time."

"It's probably wonderful conversation, only I don't know how to talk it." I was beginning to know what Wild, Pen, Buddy, and these other kids were like. They drove Allards and Jags, sat around big, comfortable rooms, drank beer because they liked beer, and if they liked champagne they'd drink that. If the men went to Korea and were sergeants with a line company they'd be damn good sergeants, but mostly they'd be lieutenants and a surprising lot of them would get killed being damn good lieutenants.

Wild and Pen were their kind of women, good-looking and reckless and very bright.

Yeah, I could dig these crazy kids, a little bit.

Wild was still looking at me, with friendly compassion now. "We're all waiting, not patiently, for somebody to smooth out our Buddy. I think we'd chip in for a small loving cup to the man who did it." She turned her glass in her hands. "But Buddy would come back and kill the man that whipped him. Kill him or die trying."

The record was Billie Holiday now and her voice conquered the room.

"I'm going to have to try your Buddy again."

"Why? No point, is there?" she said. "He's too fast, too hard, too mean. Why get hurt? And if you did take him, what add does that give?"

"I have to do it, for one thing. I'm going to live around here, so I'll be running into him. I'm going to have to stop that laugh of his. And there's you."

"So there is." Her eyes went over me as if she were seeing me for the first time.

Billie Holiday's voice was with us like the wind and the beat of a heart.

"Let's you and me get out of here. Let's you and me go someplace now."

"Why not?" she said, and she swung around and up like a dancer.

I got up from the floor. I felt shaky and there were plenty of aches in me.

"Where, for example?" she asked, but she was walking toward the open door and the little flight of stone steps. The others paid no attention to us.

"Bar?" I followed her through the tangle of vines and bushes outside the little house.

She turned to look at me in the bright sunshine, a tall girl in a loose gray-green coat and a soft yellow skirt, a tall girl with tiger-gold hair and the softest, clearest eyes I had ever seen.

She smiled and it was a pretty kid-sister smile, white teeth and red lips, eyes suddenly bright and crinkles at the corner of her mouth. For a moment she wasn't beautiful, only sweet and lively, the kind of girl a man wants to be with, laughing with him at funny things.

I pulled her to me and kissed her. She gave a little in that kiss, gave a little both of the pretty kid sister and of a wild, passionate woman. Both, like a touch of sweet cream and a touch of brandy.

She looked up at me—not much. I'm barely six feet—and laughed.

"Jim Work, the boy with impulses," she said. "He gets in fights, he kisses girls, he has an interesting life."

"What's this Brown? What's he mean to you, Wild?"

"He's my man. He's funny and he's a nuisance. He doesn't have a lot, but then he has me."

Take off, Work, I thought. You're in the wrong ball game. They pitch too fast and they play different rules. Take off, Pal."

"Let's take my car," said Wild.

"Which?" But I knew. It was the Nash-Healey.

"Where?" she said. She was behind the wheel in one smooth movement.

It was a word game, so I said, "Why?" and she laughed again.

"Because maybe I've got plans for you." She tooled the low

gray car down the narrow driveway to the black-top road.

"And what kind?" The car had a machinist's beauty that made me almost forget her.

"A drink, maybe two, and I'll make up my mind. You probably won't go for it.

"I'll go for it."

She took the car through the little hills to the highway and over the ridge down to Monterey, a town nothing much like Carmel-by-the-Sea. Monterey was a fishermen's town once when Steinbeck was writing about Cannery Row; now it's a tourists' town and a soldiers' town, but still a good, pleasant place.

We hadn't said anything during the short drive from the Zoo to Tyler Street in Monterey. Wild was the kind of girl that enjoyed driving. I had nothing to say. My face and body still hurt, Wild had kissed me and then told me she belonged to Buddy Brown.

I was thinking: You fall in what you feel may be love damn fast, in minutes, maybe in seconds and there's no future to it.

"Are you married, Jim?" Wild was backing into an open space by the curb; this was the first thing she had said since we left Carmel.

"No. I'm just a broken-down G.I. college student."

"What do you like to do?" The Healey was parked now.

"What I'm doing. Just living."

She slid out of the car. "How's for the Mission Inn for our drinks?"

"Good." I knew the place. For three weeks I'd been getting to know the bars of the Peninsula, and this was a pleasant one—a small room with a prow-shaped bar and quite a lot of action, one big room with tables and quite a lot of comfort. We went into the big room, Wild sat down, and I went into the little room to get us some beer.

As I came back into the spacious room I looked at Wild. I saw a beautiful young girl sitting at a big table, her short, bronze-gold hair still ruffled from the wind. She saw an ordinary guy in jacket, sport shirt, and slacks, his face swollen, carrying two bottles of beer. We were alone in the big room and for a moment we looked at each other and somehow we knew each other in that moment.

She was looking surprised, then thoughtful, as I set down

the two bottles and the two glasses. I poured her beer and dropped into the low-backed chair next to her.

"Do you know much about people like Pen, Smoky, Buddy, me—the rest of us?"

"Why are you asking, Wild?"

"You know why." That was the way she told me that she, too, had known what that meeting of eyes had meant.

I nodded. "I think I know something about you, Wild." I looked away. "What were these plans?"

"Plans?" She was thinking about things somewhere else, maybe that other dimension her kind of people live in.

"You said you had plans for me and I wouldn't like them."

She looked at me in a new way now, as if she were trying to see me as someone else might see me.

"I have to know a little bit about you first, Jim."

I shrugged. "There's not much. Chicago boy. Drafted two years ago. Sergeant with a line outfit in Korea. Signed up at Monterey Peninsula College when I got out three weeks ago. I'd never seen this part of the country before and I liked it fine. I don't know anybody here, I've got that Ford you saw, and I'm staying at a motel out on Fremont. Anything else?"

"What did you do before you were drafted?"

"Fooled around a little bit with television. I had a low-echelon job with an outfit that made TV films. They folded while I was in the Land of Morning Calm."

"Family?"

"Folks died in a car smash-up six years ago. Relatives in Chicago, nothing else."

"This is an odd question: What kind of drinker are you?"

I laughed. "If they'll sell it and I've got the money to buy it, I'll drink it. Nothing big. Beer mostly."

She nodded. "You look like a nice steady beer drinker. Temper?"

"Not as hot as your sweet man's."

"You're allowed about two strikes. You've just taken one." Her eyes were cool, her lips slightly parted.

"You allow me no strikes. You allow me nothing. I'm going along with your questions and—" I stopped. She had me and I'd been as gawky and obvious as I'd been at sixteen. "Sure. O.K."

"Thanks, Jim. Don't throw rocks at me. This is serious for

me."

She reached across the table and took my hand. Hers was strong and warm with long, slender fingers and unpolished, well-groomed nails.

"I'm going to ask you a crazy favor and I think you'll be smart if you say sorry, but you're too busy. One more thing: Do you go the sticks route at all?"

"Sticks? You mean marijuana?"

She nodded.

"No. I saw a little of it in Chicago, a little in Tokyo. Not my style."

"That about does it, Jim. You're what I need, if you'll go."

"What going do I do?"

"Last night my father wired me from New York. He'll be here this evening—flying from New York to San Francisco and then taking a local plane down to Monterey. He's due at the airport about five-twenty."

"So?"

"So he knows I've got a man. He called me long-distance last week at eight o'clock in the morning, New York time."

"That's five here. A touch early."

"Pen answered, all knocked out with sleep. She didn't know who it was and she mumbled just enough so that my father realized I was out somewhere with some boy."

"This did things to him?"

"Not so much. He just wants to see the boy and make sure I'm not with bad people. He realizes I'm twenty-two, I've got a body. I'm somewhat pleasant to know, so a lot of boys and men try their luck with me. Somebody's bound to make out. He knows that."

"What about marriage?" There was a lot of sense to what she had said, but it wasn't the kind of pattern for living much in use back home.

"I like the way I live. I'm no wife now, maybe I'll never be a wife. At this curve in my road I don't see what I can give marriage or marriage can give me."

"Kind of selfish, aren't you, Wild?"

"That wasn't your second strike. Just a pop foul. How about some more beer?"

I walked back to the little room with the bar where the

crowd was people I could understand, men with business in the neighborhood, reporters from the Herald, girls who worked and were having Martinis on a Saturday afternoon. The barman passed my beers to me and I walked to Wild. I knew what she wanted me to do and I knew I was going to do it.

Chapter Three

"Why not have him meet Buddy Brown? Are you ashamed of him?" I poured her beer, and it foamed up and over the glass, puddling on the table. We were still alone in the big, quiet room.

She looked up at me. "It's a fair question, Jim. I'm not ashamed of him, but my father will know him. Not his name or who he is. Hell know what he is."

I sat down and looked at her sensitive, beautiful face.

"He'll look at him and know him. The kind of guy that has talent and feeling, maybe even has ability, but who buried all that a long time ago. The kind of guy who's a bad drunk, who borrows and cheats for money to live on, who beats up strangers at bars and parties because he's able to whip most men, who always has some woman like me around, most of the time three or four. A guy who likes marijuana, a liar, a useless guy, slightly psycho."

"Your guy," I said.

"My guy now. Not a month ago, maybe not a month from now. Right today, yes."

"And this particular stranger who got beat up by your man—what about me?"

"You're the man I take to my father."

"Why?"

"Why for you, or why for me?"

"Both."

"For me because I'm my father's daughter. I don't want him to feel sorry for me."

"I understand. Some of it, anyway."

"As for you, Jim, you'd be doing me a favor. I know you're going to do it and I know why. There's nothing much I can say about it."

I nodded. "That's it. "What do I say to your father?"

"Nothing much. He'll look at you and he'll know pretty close to right what you are. I think he'll like it and he won't be sorry for me."

"So you say. Supposing he's a little annoyed that I've been

bundling with his lovely blonde daughter and starts throwing his weight around?"

"No."

"I'll take the chance. And Buddy?"

"If he finds out, he'll think it's very funny."

"Great sense of humor, your Buddy."

She finished her glass of beer.

"Before we go to the airport you'd better fill me in. How long have we been playing house?"

She pressed her lips. "Three weeks."

"I met you the night I left Fort Ord, then, a free man. Where?"

"Mission Ranch."

"O.K. I know the place. And why did you go for me?"

"I liked you."

"What are our plans together?"

She shook her head. "My father won't ask that."

"Who or what is your father, by the way?"

"He's just a man. Office in New York. Our home is in Westport. Divorced my mother years ago. She's been in Europe most of the time. He has quite a lot of money."

It was a quarter to five. "Let's go." I said.

We walked to the gray car and got in. She handled it as if she loved it. It was all smooth, all gliding, all with power and speed. She was a gentleman behind the wheel, but a gentleman who was sure and confident. The heavy traffic on the road to the airport meant nothing to her and the gray car.

We didn't talk. I was conscious of her being there and my nerves were hot wires; this wouldn't be something to write off as a mixed-up afternoon. The smooth arms as she held the wheel, the ripple as she moved them, the long legs riding the pedals.

We were twenty minutes early at the airport and it was good. Somehow we found a cool closeness over a table in the airport cafe. Coffee and talk.

We talked about a book we'd both read a couple of years back, "The Catcher in the Rye." We both loved it. And "The Caine Mutiny." Pictures. Both of us were solid for Alec Guinness, and we liked swimming, walking just to walk, riding. She could ski, I wanted to.

That kind of talk.

It was fine and I could feel what it was doing to me. I find the girl who looks and acts the way I've always wanted the girl to look and act, then I find she's a girl who enjoys life the way I do. What more? She's Wild Kearny and she's in love with Buddy Brown and I'm going to meet her father in a couple of minutes, because his plane is circling in now, and pretend to be the boy she's been living with.

We walked out to meet him. The ship came in smoothly, taxied around, and came to a stop about fifty feet from us.

He was the first man out. Wild said, "Father," as he stepped out on the stairs.

We stood there and watched him come toward us, Wild holding my hand. He was a big man and he looked like an important man, from the way he carried himself and the kind of clothes he wore.

I recognized him just before he reached us. His picture has been in Time and True had run a story on him. It was easy to understand what Wild had meant when she'd said her father wouldn't feel sorry for her if he met me instead of Buddy Brown. It was also easy to understand how much of a jam Wild had set up for me. Her father was Broadway Red Kearny.

Red hair mixed with iron gray. Six feet two, 220 pounds, with the broadest shoulders I have ever seen. Red face and ice-blue eyes. Broadway Red Kearny.

Wild loved him, you could see that. She threw her arms around him and stretched up for a kiss. There were a few moments when father and daughter were alone and there was no one else in all the world. Then he turned away from her to me and they were individuals again, the lovely girl with the tiger-gold hair and the big man with the ice-blue eyes, Wild Kearny and Broadway Red Kearny.

He had once killed two of Joe Adonis' troopers in a Fifty-second Street night club. He was acquitted because two hoods had had their guns and Broadway Red had had only his bare hands.

The ice-blue eyes met mine, and it was like picking up a bare 220-volt lead. You felt the vitality and the power of this big man, his knowledge and judgment of men, his ruthlessness, his justice. He didn't hold out his hand to me; we looked at each other.True magazine had told of how Broadway Red had once knocked down big Jimmy Dorich in a sudden flare of anger one night at Toots Shor's. That was when Jimmy was the toughest detective on the Broadway beat and a tough man in a fight. They shook hands five minutes later.

The big man didn't make up his mind about me. I wasn't in, nor was I out. He wasn't sure about the man his daughter had brought to the airport, a kind of ordinary guy but one whose eyes had met and held his. We both looked at Wild at the same time.

"Is this your boy, Wild?" he asked. His voice was soft and deep.

Now it was Wild who felt the pressure, and I knew that she had not told many lies to this big, soft-voiced man who loved her. She was going to tell one now and she despised herself.

"This is Jim Work," she said, and the lie was unspoken but there.

"My name is Kearny, Work, and that's the way we'll talk to each other."

"Right, Kearny," I said.

Broadway Red, last of the big gamblers, straight, smart, tough. He was not in the Syndicate, but the little rats of the Big Combination scuttled when he came by, because he had his troops too, fast, merciless gunmen from the dockworkers' local that he controlled, the local that he had built when he was a brawling longshoreman thirty years before. Most trouble Broadway Red could handle with his powerful hands, but the rats knew that if anyone dared cut down Broadway Red, his boys would hunt the lords of the Syndicate and slaughter them, in East New York, along the West Side, in Brownsville and Miami, in Las Vegas and Beverly Hills. The writer in the magazine had shown a respect for the man that you seldom find for any man who walks today on Broadway or across on Fifty-second.

"You feel like eating?" he asked.

"I think I could chew on a live wolf right now."

"Steak, Red?" said Wild.

"Is there any other kind of food proper for men?"

"Let's go to the Hearthstone, Jim," she said, and she couldn't meet my eyes as she spoke to me. I hoped her father didn't notice.

The three of us got into the Healey, and it was a tight squeeze. I was against Broadway Red's biceps and they were big and rock-hard. This was a lot of man.

It was getting dark and the bright warmth of the day was gone when Wild parked the car on the main street of Carmel. We walked to the Hearthstone, a simple, pleasant place where they have good, big charcoal-broiled steaks.

As we followed the host to our table, I saw the other diners turn to look at Kearny. Ordinarily both men and women would have turned to look at the blonde perfection of Wild, but with her father there they looked at him and wondered who he was. He was used to the turning heads; he walked with a curious softness and a gentleness.

It was sirloin for Wild and me, porterhouse for Broadway Red. After the steaks he ordered brandy, and it was over the brandy that he talked to us.

"You're a grown woman, Wild." There was a sudden flash of rebellion across her face and I thought I could understand a little of this father and his daughter. She loved and idolized this man, but she had to find her own love in a man, a man who could somehow humble and defeat the power of her father. In some perverse, night-haunted way, this might have led her to the lean evil of Buddy Brown.

"You're a grown woman," he repeated, "and right now you're fine and pretty and full of pride."

He took two cigars from his coat pocket and offered me one. They were cased in aluminum with no brand name, probably his own specials. I lit his with my lighter and I noticed him glance at the regimental crest on it. We both sent out clouds of blue smoke, and Wild sipped her brandy.

"You've seen some of the girls at Palm Beach, up in Maine during the summer, around midtown New York," he went on, and there was still a touch of brogue in his speech. He was talking to Wild, but he wanted me to listen, too. "The beautiful girls a few years older than you are now. You've seen them, and you must have noticed the little lines, the little hardness in their eyes, the meanness around their mouths."

He took a drink of brandy.

"I've been watching the lovely girls change for many, many years, and it's not a pretty sight. They're fresh and fine like you now, and then, little by little, they're neither fresh nor fine any more. You've seen them, Wild, and you know what I mean.

"I don't want that to happen to you. I'd rather see you get big and fat, with round arms and red hands, like my mother, and have the look on your face my mother had. Life was a good thing to her, hard but good. Not the emptiness that these girls know. I don't want to see your eyes get so hard they don't see any good in things any more."

Wild was watching him and I could see that she knew what he meant.

"You've got everything in your hands now, and it can all turn to sand on you and run through your fingers before you even know it. Maybe I'm going to be making a mistake now, but at least it will be an honest mistake."

"This man has been good enough for you to want, and I don't blame him for wanting you. Good or bad, strong or weak, you've given him the one thing that only you could give him. Maybe there've been others, maybe you're cursed with hot blood like your Aunt Kitty, I don't know and I pray not. But now you're old enough and smart enough to pick your man, and you've picked him. So you're going to be married to him."

Wild and I looked at each other. He watched us with those ice-blue eyes.

"I'll give you nothing but my blessings. A young man and a young woman should want nothing more than each other and what they can make of life together, and that's the way it'll be for you two. I'll give you no money. If the young man wants a job, I'll see that he gets one fitting his abilities and no more.

"If you love each other and do well together, if the Lord sends you children and you're happy, in a year or two I'll make it different. Then you'll have the best and lots of the best because I'll know you deserve it. Not until then.

"But married you'll be, and by a priest, and as soon as I can arrange it, which will be soon indeed. You're not Catholic, are you, Work?"

"No, Kearny, I'm not."

"D'you have any objection to being married within the Catholic Church, assuming of course that we can satisfy the priest as to the Tightness of it?"

I had several choices. I could explain the truth and that

would be the end of that, not only for Wild and me, but maybe for Wild and her father. I could keep on pretending to be Wild's man and try to wiggle out of this sudden marriage. I could go along with Broadway Red and marry his daughter.

I looked at Wild again and tried to guess what decision she was making. We had met each other less than four hours ago.

Somewhere, probably not far away, was Buddy Brown.

Chapter Four

"I've already asked your daughter to marry me," I said quietly. Odd, I had a quick picture of a junior-college football game—me with the ball and three big mugs from the other team converging on me. I had tossed a lateral. This time the lateral was to Wild Kearny.

The big man's eyes were hard on me, deep into me. Inside of me, somewhere, I must have been telling more truth than lie, because he was satisfied.

"That's a good thing to hear, Jim," he said, and then he looked at his daughter.

"And I will have none of it." Wild's voice was low. "I am a grown woman, as you say. When I give the vows of marriage it will be because I mean them, because I want to give them."

"You don't want to marry Jim?"

"Every girl adds up a column of mistakes," she answered, her clear eyes looking into his, "and I'd rather have a lot of little mistakes than one big one."

His voice was softer than ever now and the brogue was stronger, and these were signs of anger. "They weren't big mistakes that turned those pretty girls' mouths and eyes hard and mean, it was year after year of little mistakes. You'll marry Jim Work and that's the end of it. You'll be a good wife or you'll be no daughter of mine!"

"I'm the man," I said, "and as the man I've got something to say. When Wild wants me, we'll be married. Not before."

His big hand closed on my wrist. There was iron strength there.

"And until then you'll toss her on her bottom, and afterward you'll tip your hat and be on your way whistlin'. Is that the way of it?"

Wild stood up, and she was as angry as Broadway Red.

"Here are the keys to the car you gave me for my birthday. You've forgotten it was my twenty-first, I think. As for your money, I don't want it. As for your advice, I don't need it. Go back to New York, where you can boss people around. You won't boss me!" The keys hit the table and she strode out of the restaurant.

We watched her go, each of us with his own thoughts.

His fingers left my wrist. "That's the way of it," he said.

We were silent, and then he said, "Who's been working on your face, Jim?"

"I had a fight."

"Win?"

"Lost."

He didn't say anything, but I don't think he'd lost any fights in his fifty years. Not by anybody's rules.

"What will we do about our girl, Jim?"

"We'll work it out. Wild and I."

"It won't be like that." The soft voice had power in it now, not loud, not hurried. "I came here to see her married. Either that or break the neck of her man."

His hands were before me, open, the fingers ready. They were well manicured, but still the stubby fingers of a longshoreman, a bare-fist fighter, a killer.

"If he hadn't been a man, if he hadn't the right stuff in him—But no matter. I'm satisfied with you. I'll take the two of you to the church and then you'll be on your own. If you do well I'll see that you do better."

The big fists closed again on my wrists.

"Now we'll go out and find her, and if I have to I'll carry her under my arm to the wedding, but a wedding there'll be. If you give me trouble, I'll give you the back of my hand till the teeth fly out of your mouth."

I put a twenty on the waiter's plate. It was one of my last six twenties but I wanted to pay this tab. Not to impress Kearny. Those weren't the things that meant anything to him. I just wanted to pay this one.

"What do you do, boy?"

"Three weeks out of the Army. Korea."

"An officer?"

"A sergeant."

He nodded. "And what kind of a sergeant, Jim?"

"Line outfit. Infantry. Nothing fancy."

"What are you going to do?"

"Go to college here. It's a good chance to go."

I was reckless, angry, ashamed. Lying to this proud, red bear of a man, pretending something that I wanted to be true, and knowing there was nothing there.

The waiter brought the change. I left a couple of bucks, and we got up.

"You're sullen, boy. Why?"

I looked at him, looked into the cold ice-blue eyes.

"You're Broadway Red Kearny," I said. "You're big, tough, and rich. I'm not big, not tough, not rich. My name's Jim Work and I stopped taking orders three weeks ago."

He chuckled. "And more power to you. In everything except this marriage. Here are the keys to her car. Let's find her."

Outside I fumbled around a little and then got it started.

It was quite a feeling to drive the gray car. It felt different than any car I'd ever driven before, lighter, surer, quicker. Wild must have been plenty angry to toss the keys to it back to her father.

I had a fair idea of where the Zoo was, but only a fair idea. Carmel is full of private village jokes—no street numbers, no street lights. I'd have to poke around up and down the black streets until I found the right little vine-covered cottage in a good-sized town made up of hundreds of vine-covered cottages.

After five minutes or so Broadway Red asked, "Where are you going, lad?"

"Wild's house. It's around here somewhere."

"Boy, stop the car." There was something to the big man's voice that made you decide not to argue. I swung the car over to the side of the road.

"Why have you been lying to me?"

I didn't say anything.

"You didn't know how to start her car. You aren't sure of where she lives. You've acted like a stranger in a family quarrel. You're not the boy she's been fooling with, are you?"

"No, I'm not. I met her this afternoon." That felt right. You don't like to lie or act a lie to men like Broadway Red Kearny.

Now he was silent for a long time. I felt sorry for the big guy.

"Who is the fellow? Do you know him?"

"I've met him."

"Why did you pretend to be him?"

"I just sort of got into it."

"She asked you to do it."

I didn't say anything. There are two kinds of relationship that are strong. One is the thing I had for Wild Kearny, and there's a loyalty, a pride, and an understanding in it. Or there should be. The other is one between men as men, and I could feel that with Broadway Red Kearny. Not exactly friendship, we weren't friends. Maybe a dignity, something that has to be honest and straight or you feel that you're cheating and weak.

"Why did she?" His voice was soft, very low. "Why did you say you'd asked her?"

"I'm not sure."

"Something wrong with this man of hers?"

"I don't know."

"Do you think you can find her place?"

"I'll try."

About two minutes later the headlights picked out a driveway, then gleamed over my Ford. The Jaguar was gone but the MG was there. I pulled up behind it, turned off the ignition, and handed the keys to Kearny.

"That's my car there. Nice to have met you. See you around." I got out.

"Jim." The big man climbed out of the Nash-Healey.

"Yes?"

"Running out?"

"I never was in."

"I see. All right, Work." I had liked having him call me "Jim."

And I was still in this on a double count. I wanted to tangle with Buddy again. And I had a feeling about Wild that wasn't quite being in love with her, the way diving off the high board isn't quite being in the water—but you can see it in front of you, coming up fast.

"Probably nobody in there wants to see me, but I'll go in with you," I said.

"As you say, Jim."

I led the way down the three stone steps and pushed open the door. There was a record playing. Gerry Mulligan maybe.

Buddy Brown was holding Wild in his arms. Her head was back, her body tight to his. If we had come a few minutes later it might have been a little rough on everybody. It was plenty rough on me just the way it was. There was no sense to my wild blaze of jealousy, but sense had nothing to do with it.

Wild must have taken a cab and come straight here and Buddy must have been waiting for her. They heard Kearny close the door and they turned to look at us.

I wanted to say, "Hello punk," to Buddy, to try him again, right there and then. But up behind my eyes something was saying, play it cool. You'll look like a jerk and he'll probably take you in three punches.

I said, "Hello, Wild. Hello, punk."

"What did you do? Bring your old man?" Then he sensed the tension between the girl and the big man.

"Oh, wrong old man. Hi there, Red."

Kearny walked across the floor and hit Buddy Brown in the face. The tall, thin boy crashed back into a chair, toppling it over, and rolled to the floor.

"You'll call me Mr. Kearny when you speak to me."

Wild looked at her father for one blazing second and then she went to Buddy. He was trying to get up and blood was spurting out of his nose, trickling from his mouth.

He made it up but he was shaky. He took the white handkerchief from his breast pocket and wiped at his face, pushing Wild away from him with his left hand.

"All right, slugger, all right," he said thickly. Wild dropped her hands to her sides and stood there. The room was a kind of stage now with three of us standing there, Kearny, Wild, Work, and the spotlight on the tall, pale-faced boy wiping the blood from his face. Buddy Brown had that trick of being the center, the one the rest watched.

The Gerry Mulligan record ended, the player buzzed, and it was the old Artie Shaw again.

Buddy Brown straightened his shoulders, crumpled the bloody handkerchief into a ball, and threw it into the fireplace. Then he walked by Kearny and me, up the three steps, and into the darkness outside. Wild watched him go, her hands still at her sides.

None of us said anything. We heard the whir of the MG's starter and the rustle as its tires spun on the gravel and dirt.

"That was your man?" Kearny asked.

"Yes."

"I'll go now," I said. Nobody answered. I felt awkward and stiff-legged as I turned and left the room.

I closed the front door behind me, walked over to my Ford, got in, and started it. I backed it down the dark driveway, curving around the Nash-Healey, and drove out into the street. The MG was parked there, its motor running. I recognized it in the blackness by its headlights, low and close together.

I straightened out the Ford and headed toward the road to Monterey. The MG followed. That was fine with me.

Chapter Five

Saturday-night traffic was a river of light over the hill and down to Monterey. I would have looked back over the whole crazy afternoon and evening, picked over the jagged pieces, but they scattered in my mind; because what I was thinking about was the man following me.

I didn't try to lose him but he took no chances. The close, low lights of the MG were never more than twenty yards behind me, sometimes as close as five. I turned off Munras and went down Tyler to the Mission Inn. The MG pulled up to the curb along the now nearly empty street barely twenty feet from where I parked.

He was waiting for me when I got out of my Ford.

"Don't shoot, boy," he said to me. "I want to kiss and make up."

"So?" We were alone on the dim street. The Mission Inn was bright enough, but the doorway to the bar was solid and the only light came from three portholes in it.

"I lost a one-punch hassle back there. You're probably satisfied, and I want to talk to you."

If I told Buddy Brown that I didn't want to talk to him I'd sound like a sulking kid. If I swung on him I'd be in a street fight and not at all sure what I was fighting for. Those were the only choices that occurred to me.

I said, "Why?"

"You came back with that overage slugger."

"Yeah?"

"I want to talk to you about Wild." He held out his hand. "Let's have a drink."

I didn't take his hand but I pushed open the heavy door that led to the little barroom of the Mission Inn and held it for him. He went through and I followed.

Henry, the evening barman, looked up as we came in, and after a moment he smiled a little. I knew Henry slightly from visits during the past three weeks; he was a very sharp and observant guy.

"Third round over?" he asked. He was a beach-browned man who looked much like a Spanish nobleman. I didn't understand the "third round" thing until I saw Brown's face. His mouth was swollen, and so was mine. Both of us looked a little beat up. Both of us were.

"Beer here, Henry. You?" I looked at Buddy.

He nodded. "Roll you for them," he said, reaching for two dice boxes.

We rolled and I won. Brown paid for the two beers, reaching into his pocket and pulling out a few bills, mostly fives, wadded together.

"Let's sit back where it's quiet," he said.

I was a little curious about Brown's sudden interest in me, and though the two of us were apparently natural-born enemies, the kind of men who fight on sight, I took my bottle and glass into the big room where Wild and I had sat hours earlier. It wasn't empty now. A fair man and a big, handsome dark-haired woman were drinking highballs at one table, at another a very fat sergeant was smoking a pipe and playing chess with a harassed-looking middle-aged man who had a big nose and shell-framed glasses.

"Now what?" I said to Buddy when we were seated at a table in the corner.

"You met Wild for the first time today? When we tangled cars?"

I nodded.

"But you knew Broadway Red before?"

"No."

His eyes were black, bright, and hard in his white face. He didn't believe me.

"Does he know she's hooked?"

I looked at him. I knew what he meant, but I didn't believe it of Wild Kearny. Not that clear-eyed, proud girl. He bent toward me, sitting loose in his chair, a lanky, long-boned, sinewy man, his swollen mouth still twisted into a mocking half-smile.

"I don't believe it."

"Do you think I'm hooked?"

I looked into his shining eyes, at his white face, at his hands.

"No. I've seen men on heroin and morphine. Not many, but

some. You're not on that stuff. Marijuana, sure, but nothing that would hook you."

"You're real smart."

As long as the two of us were within sight of each other, we were set to go. I had to let him move first, but I hated it, because his first move would be something I might not expect, maybe a beer bottle in my face. I was tense and my hands were cold again.

"I'm trying to find out if you know Broadway Red or not. You say not, and probably you're a real honest boy. But still— Broadway Red is a little bit important to me."

We looked at each other. It's a hard thing to say you want to kill a man, but I've killed men—strangers in quilted uniforms in the early mist on the Punchbowl ridges; killed two carefully and slowly with my Ml, killed one in a panic fight, smashing his skull with the butt of my Ml. I wanted to kill Buddy Brown and I was angry with knowing that he didn't care one way or the other about me. He might kill me, but not because he hated me more than any other man. He didn't, and the burden of hatred was all mine.

"You don't know Broadway Red at all, maybe you've never been to New York, stuff like that?" Buddy asked again, spinning his glass between his slender fingers.

I looked across the table into his mocking face. "This has been a goof-off afternoon for me. From the time you cut in front of me in Carmel to right now it's been goof-off. You want to talk, Buddy, let's talk. You don't want to talk, then let's go back in the alley and try it again. O.K. with you?"

He lit a cigarette before he answered. "You're a real hairpin, boy. Always willing. I like that about you. But I don't want to fight you. I'm your friend. Like a fraternity brother. You just keep calling me Buddy, because that's what I am—your buddy, buddy."

This was the man who had Wild. This was the man she was ashamed to show to her father because she knew that Broadway Red would pity her, seeing Buddy Brown.

"Let's talk like a couple of friends," Buddy went on. "About music. Maybe you like Dixieland. You're probably a real Dixieland fiend. Or maybe we can talk about sports cars, and you can tell me how you're saving up to buy a Jag or a Riley.

But then, you're probably a Cadillac man. Then we can get down to talking about women. You like blonde girls, kind of tall?

Maybe you're saving up to get a blonde girl. Let me give you the word, don't bother. I've got some spares, I'll loan you one. I'm your buddy."

"Broadway Red get you kind of mad, Buddy?"

He waited a moment or two. "That's right. It upsets me to have some old gentleman give me a Sunday punch in front of you and the blonde. It upsets me so much that I'm probably not very good company, am I boy?"

"You're a punk."

"You keep calling me that, boy, but you don't stand up to it very good. I'll tell you something. I'm going to make you crawl across the dirt to me begging me not to hurt you any more. Crawling and begging. Can you see it? Is it a picture to you?"

"Let's go back to the alley."

He laughed. His left hand snaked across the table and he had the second finger of my right hand in his fist, bending it back, holding my palm hard against the table. His right hand thrust his cigarette toward my eyes and I ducked my head back. Still torturing my finger with his left hand hard on my right, he moved up like a cat and his fingers laced into my short hair. He pulled my head way back and I tried to reach him with my left hand. He let go and clipped me across the throat with the side of his right hand. A hard clip on the Adam's apple.

It was all pain. I couldn't breathe. I couldn't move. I was in the chair, my head hanging forward, loose, holding myself up on my elbows. I could see the puddles of beer on the tabletop, I could feel the frantic pounding of my heart.

Maybe nobody noticed. It happened inside of ten seconds. I was sick and weak, knowing only the ultimate desperation of trying to get air through my paralyzed throat to my lungs.

He didn't say anything until he thought I could hear him again. Then he said, "You're probably a good man, a real good man, fighting boys like yourself. Don't feel bad. You don't have it, that's all. In about five minutes you'll be able to talk again. Then we'll talk about Broadway Red, where you met him, how well you know him. Then we'll talk about Wild, about how she's crazy about me. Then we'll go to some quiet place and I'll work you over until you crawl to me. Then we'll say good-by and that will be the end of our friendship. You can write to me if you want to."

I was there in the chair, my head hanging forward, the pain easing a little.

Somebody had walked up to the table. "Is your friend all right?" It sounded like Henry's voice.

"He choked on something. Swallowed his beer wrong."

"You all right?" It was Henry. I tried to look up at him. I nodded.

He stood there a moment, uncertain, and then he walked away.

Buddy Brown spoke to me softly. "Probably now you're thinking about getting a gun or a knife, or jumping me from behind. Think nice thoughts, boy. After I'm through with you you won't think about those things. Just hearing my name will make you cry and try to hide. Do you know why I'm going to do that to you?"

I was able to lift my head now. I looked at him.

"Because you like to call me a punk."

This was a nightmare worse than any lonely night in the quiet, deadly darkness of Korea. I was all hate, and anger, sick and weak; he was talking to me in a low voice and laughing at me.

"You won't get rid of me tonight, boy. I'll be with you until I'm through with you. You want to ask the police for help, boy? Something like that? Are you scared, boy?"

This snake-quick sadist had me. Three times today he'd taken me, knocked me down, kicked me, hurt me. I had forgotten Wild now, forgotten everything except the hate and the fear that were like bitter ice in my blood.

"You're not one of Broadway Red's people. You're not tough enough or smart enough." Buddy had brought his face close to mine. "But you met him somewhere tonight and brought him to Wild's house. What is he on the Coast for? Where is he staying?"

The glittering eyes were deadly intent now.

I guessed that Wild had told him nothing of her father. He hadn't known that Kearny was flying west. Yet he had recognized him almost at once and now he wanted information. Information about a man who had deadly enemies.

The first time I tried to say something there was no voice at all and my throat tightened with a sudden aching. After half a minute I tried again, and produced only a hoarse squawk. I didn't have anything to say, anyway. All I wanted to do was get out of there, away from Buddy Brown.

There was a sound of quick steps across the wooden floor.

"Hello, Buddy. Buy me a drink?"

I turned and saw Pen Brooks.

"Hi, kid. How'd you find me?"

"I saw your car and I peeked in the window."

"Great." Buddy smiled. "We're busy. Take off."

Pen Brooks pushed back the empty chair at the table and sat in it. She was a pretty girl, not striking but with good eyes, a good mouth, a good body. Some nice family's nice daughter, a Pasadena kind of girl.

"I said take off, Brooks." Buddy was still smiling.

Pen looked at me. "Oh, hello. I thought you two were feuding and making muscles at each other." Then she looked at Buddy. Then hungry desperation was pitifully open. "I've been looking all over for you."

"Did you just come from the Zoo?"

"A little while ago. Then I drove around Carmel looking for your car. I tried Monterey and there it was. You'd be surprised how far away I can spot your car, Buddy.

"Who was at the Zoo?"

"Wild."

"Who else?"

Pen Brooks hesitated. "Her father."

"You knew he was coming. Why didn't you tell me?" The snarl and the smile were both there now.

"We haven't been together in three days, Buddy."

"You should have told me this afternoon."

"Wild asked me not to tell you."

Her hands were across the table on his wrists, the fingers grasping at him. She was either a little drunk or high on marijuana.

"Listen, Brooks, go out and pick up some boy somewhere. If he isn't sure you're worth the price of a motel, have him call me and I'll tell him you're great. Now get out of here."

"Buddy." Pen Brooks's mouth was imploring. "Buddy, I'll meet you somewhere later. Anywhere. I've got plenty of money,

Buddy. Please."

A pretty girl from a nice family. This afternoon at the Zoo with the three boys she had looked so right, as if she found the world a pleasant place of young men who drove Jaguars and played good golf and liked Gerry Mulligan records and drank beer and eventually married nice, pretty girls.

"Get out of here, bum, or I'll throw you out." Buddy was still smiling.

Pen looked at me. She laughed, pretending to me, to Buddy, to herself, that this was all fun, boy-and-girl insults given in laughing sophistication.

She got up. "Well, if you won't buy me a drink, where'll you be later, Buddy? Mission Ranch, maybe?"

"Get out of here, bum."

She smiled and walked out, head high.

Chapter Six

"You told that cop today that you'd been a soldier. Just got back from Korea." Brown lit another cigarette. I watched him, trying to gauge the strength that was coming back slowly to my body as the ache in my throat eased. This was strange—to know that I'd met the man that was the final one to me, the one you killed or died trying to kill. Met him the same day that I'd met the girl I wanted for the rest of my life. I wondered if he had called her "bum"—yet.

"When you were in Korea you probably thought lots about women. You're young and healthy, no girls around much over there, you probably thought lots about them. Too bad I didn't know you so I could write you letters and send you pictures. Now tell me about Broadway Red."

I stood up.

"Sit down, boy."

I knew I wasn't ready to try Buddy Brown yet. A hard blow to the throat is a bad one to take, paralyzing, strangling, and you don't come out of it quickly. I walked through the door to the smaller room, still alive with talk and laughter. There were half a dozen men at the bar. Henry glanced up at me; he had the good barman's intuition about people and he had known that things weren't right. I sat on a stool.

"Brandy."

His eyebrows flickered. "Any trouble?"

"No trouble, Henry."

He poured the brandy and set the glass before me. His eyes looked beyond me, through the door to the larger room. I didn't turn around. Brown didn't follow me.

"Pardon me, but didn't we meet this afternoon?" There were two empty stools to my right and then on the last one was the boy from the Zoo, the one in the turtle-neck sweater who had helped me after Brown had worked me over back of the house. The whole damned afternoon and evening seemed to be Brown working me over.

"Yeah, you're Pete. Right?" I said. He smiled and slid over

the two stools.

"I didn't mean to seem brutal this afternoon. After that fight, I mean."

"That's all right. You helped me enough." I looked at him. He was wearing a dark blue jacket now, and narrow bow tie.

"You're Jim ..."

"Jim Work."

"And I'm Pete Barrow."

"Glad to meet you again." We shook hands.

"Sorry about that fellow Brown. He's a lot of fun, but he's got a nasty temper."

"Yeah."

"He's not really one of our crowd."

"No?"

"Wild met him a few weeks ago. He seems to have a fascination for women."

"Sure does." I looked around, bent over to get a better view into the big room. Buddy Brown was gone.

"Wild's a fine girl." He ordered another round of the same for each of us.

"I don't know her well," I said. "I'll roll you for the drinks."

"Fine."

We rolled the dice and I won.

"Pen Brooks is a fine girl." Pete's conversation seemed somewhat limited.

"She was in here a while back," I said.

"Where?" The smooth pleasantness of his good-looking face rippled for a moment.

"Back in the big room. Brown was there, too."

"With you?" He had slipped off the stool to look into the other room.

"In a way."

"They're not there now," he said. "Were you all together?"

"She just stopped by. I don't know what happened to Brown."

"Oh." He seemed to turn over his own thoughts for a while. "Pen and I are engaged." This time I said, "Oh." He hadn't been more than twenty feet away, on the other side of the wall, when Pen Brooks had been there.

"Didn't you notice Brown's MG outside?"

"This place is crawling with MG's," Pete answered. "How long ago was Pen here?"

"Ten minutes, maybe."

"Darn." He was the kind of guy who said darn. "This is the first Saturday night in weeks that Pen and I haven't had a date. She said she was going to stay at the Zoo and do some work."

"Work?"

"She's an artist. Wants to be, anyway."

"She said something about going to the Mission Ranch." It was none of my business, and when I'd said it I regretted it, but I'd been thinking about other things.

"Just by herself?" He seemed shocked.

"I don't know. Maybe she was talking about some other time."

"She's been terribly restless these last few days."

"Who is this Buddy Brown?" I asked.

Barrow shrugged. "Wild met him and brought him around. He's from Los Angeles, that's about all I know. Maybe his folks have money, but he doesn't seem quite like that. He's just around—a little golf, sports-car rallies, those things. Wild seems to like him. The rest of us take him because of her, I think."

"And Wild herself—who is she?"

His carefully tended caste consciousness buzzed on that one. Young men like Pete Barrow talk about women only to their friends. He might unbend a way to me, but he'd already set up all the friends he'd ever have, back at prep school or at Santa Barbara or at Bar Harbor and Mount Desert.

"She's from the East. Very nice girl."

That would be it from Pete Barrow. It looked to me as if Buddy had taken Pete's girl away just for practice, the way a guy like Buddy Brown will do, and apparently Pete hadn't noticed at all.

"Our crowd isn't too happy with this fellow Brown," Pete said. "He really isn't one of us. Pen wasn't with him, you say?"

"No. She just dropped by."

I wondered if Brown were waiting for me outside. He wasn't going to let me go tonight, I knew that. There was a mutual hatred between us that was extraordinary. I'd never felt that I would have to kill a man until tonight, and now, away from the guy, the feeling seemed childish and crazy. But I knew that when we saw each other again it wouldn't seem childish or crazy.

"I'll be moving on," I said to Pete.

"Good to have seen you."

I walked outside. The MG was gone. I opened the door of my Ford and she stepped out of a doorway that led to the hotel part of the Mission Inn. Pen Brooks, hurrying across the sidewalk to me, taking my arm.

"Could I talk to you?"

"Pete Barrow is in the bar there."

"Lord." She lifted her head, looking up at me. "Would you take me somewhere, anywhere, and talk to me a little bit? Please?"

"Sure. Get in."

She slid into the front seat and I walked around to the other side, got in, and started the engine. As I pulled away from the curb Pete Barrow opened the door of the bar and stood there looking at his girl and me driving away.

"I sounded pretty awful back there, didn't I?" said Pen. Somehow I had the feeling that she found a strange pride in this self-torture of hers. She hadn't seen Pete standing in the doorway, looking at us.

I shook my head. "Where to?"

"Any place. I don't want a drink. I need somebody to talk to. I don't have anybody that I can talk to. Not anybody."

The car rounded the corner to the Carmel road.

"You know a lot of people. Why me?"

"Can you explain Buddy to me? Can you?"

"What's to explain?"

"You came to the Zoo this afternoon. You and Wild and Buddy. You know about me? I'm Wild's best friend. I'm engaged to Pete. Know something else? I'm crazy about Buddy. Could you tell that Wild wasn't the only girl there this afternoon that was having a big thing with Buddy?"

"It's your life."

"Not any more. When a girl once knows Buddy, really knows him, she's like a slave. Wild pretends that she isn't, but I know better. Why is it, tell me, why is it?"

Her hand was hot on mine, dry and hot, and I could feel the nerves that made her fingers tighten in spasms.

"You tell me what he's got," I said. "You know."

"He takes off the mask. He tears off your mask. Maybe you look smug, or pretty, or cool. It's a mask. He knows it, and then you're there, and your face isn't pretty any more, or cool, or smug. Maybe you're beautiful, if passion is beautiful, but there's nothing left for you to hide behind."

It was horrible and I knew it was true.

"Nothing's really changed. I know what he is. I don't have stupid, silly plans of changing the guy. He's cruel and rotten. I love him."

"Wild talks that way too, a little. She doesn't say anything above love, though."

"She's talked to you about Buddy? What did she say?"

I was climbing the long hill to Carmel now. "The hell with it," I said. "Both of you are fascinated by a punk and you make a big thing out of it. Women have been going for his kind for a hell of a long time. Your story is no different from any of the others."

"You don't understand. I've got to do something about this tonight."

"Why?"

"I can't stand it. I've got to break off with Pete. I have to find someplace where Buddy will meet me. I don't care if he has other women."

"Why didn't you go with him in the MG instead of waiting around for me tonight?"

"Because he wouldn't let me."

"So you decided to pounce on me and make me listen to your soap-opera romance?"

"You know him. You were with him. You could tell me what to do."

"Drown yourself."

"You're a smart character, aren't you?"

"I'm sorry. It's just that you can't get me wound up about your mad passion for Brown. He and I don't get along."

"You're a little bit like him. More than Pete or the other men I know."

"Thanks."

I made the right turn to Ocean Avenue, Carmel's main street.

"Where can I drop you?" I asked. Pen Brooks had seemed like such a pretty, easygoing girl this afternoon, drinking beer and listening to records. Now she was just that worst of all nuisances, a girl telling you what a heel the guy she loves is and how much she loves him.

"Do you know where Buddy was going?"

"No, but I can tell you where Pete Barrow is."

"Where?"

"About fifty feet behind us in his Jaguar."

"Lord."

"Suppose I pull over to the curb and let you ride with him. You've got more to talk with him about than you do with me."

"Oh, Lord." Her vocabulary was a little limited. I edged over to the curb and stopped. The low, sleek Jaguar pulled up behind me. I got out, Pen stayed in my car. Pete ran up to me.

"What are you doing with Pen?" he asked.

"Turning her over to you."

He was a nice guy and he didn't know how to react. He was angry, hurt, and puzzled, so he swung on me. He was in fine physical shape and big enough, but I'd been pushed around enough for one quiet Saturday, so I stepped in close and gave him the knee. He looked terribly surprised and just for the hell of it I clipped him as he doubled up. He went over backward.

If Pen hadn't slipped in the grass she would have brained me with the heel of her shoe. The first I knew about it was when I turned to go back to the Ford and I saw a white arm in the darkness bringing something down toward my face. I ducked and she slipped. The heel of her shoe, which she was handling like a blackjack, got me on the shoulder instead of in the temple. I slapped her with my open hand and she went back. She came forward again like a fury, swinging the shoe with one hand, clawing for my eyes with the other. I batted her once more and she tumbled across Pete, her legs white in the light of the Jag's headlamps.

I went back to the Ford, feeling a little like Buddy Brown.

Chapter Seven

The fight had happened on a dark, tree-lined street, slanting downhill toward the lights and shops of Ocean Avenue, three blocks away. Other cars had gone by during the flurry but none of them had stopped.

I drove toward the lights.

What did I want? I wanted a girl, and Wild was everything I wanted in a girl. I wanted to straighten myself out about Buddy Brown. Now, away from him and alone, I felt that if I could beat him soft, smash his pale face, that would be enough. Killing a man sounds insane except when the insanity is exploding inside you.

This first afternoon with Wild had been too violent. We could never have the easy growth of love, not any more. I couldn't be the overgrown schoolboy, off to classes, looking forward to a date with his girl in the evening. In three or four years I could maybe think about marriage. Do you marry a girl like Wild Kearny?

I would.

What would she find in me? Not the evil, quick violence of Buddy Brown. Not the smooth certainties of wealth, family, and background that Pete and the other men had. She wouldn't find very much in Jim Work.

I felt lonely and empty.

I parked my car near the Pine Inn and got out. I didn't want a drink, I didn't want to talk to anybody, and I didn't want to be alone. I thought about going back to Chicago.

I went past the glitter of the shops in the Pine Inn, across the street, and on past the flutter of flames in the window fireplace of the Hearthstone. Then I saw him walking unsteadily toward me. Buddy Brown, drunk. He must have poured it down fast during the hour since I'd seen him.

"H'lo there, boy. 'Member me?" He stood there, rocking a little, his mouth half open. I had him if I wanted him. He was almost helpless.

He stood there on the light-splattered sidewalk, his long,

thin body rocking, his mouth half open and wet.

"Take off, punk," I said.

"You're right. I'm a punk. You're so right." He looked at me and there was no mockery in his face.

I started to walk by him. He put a hand on my arm.

"Don't go, boy. I have to talk to you."

"Again? You talked to me before." I pushed his hand away.

"This is serious. Dead serious. Gotta talk to you."

"About what?"

"About the mess I'm in."

"You'll always be in a mess. Big man with the babes, big man in a fight, nothing else. Take off. I want no piece of you."

"You fingered me to Red Kearny."

"You're off your rocker."

"He's gonna kill me."

"Great."

"'Strue." His hand was on my arm again, to steady himself and to hold me there. His face looked old and there was no glitter in his eyes. His voice was a soft whisper.

"So he kills you. Who weeps?" I didn't believe any of this. He was half stupid with alcohol.

I walked on down the sidewalk. He stayed with me, weaving, his hand still clutching my jacket.

"You fingered me. Now you save me and I'll give you five thousand bucks."

"You haven't got five thousand. You're crazy drunk, that's all."

"Come a li'l ways with me and I'll show you the five grand. I'll give it to you if you can save me."

"How could I save you?"

"You know Red Kearny. You found me for him. You can get me away."

"You weren't hard to find. You were on a love beat with his daughter."

"That was the big joke. That's what was so funny—until you fingered me for him."

I was beginning to get the idea that somewhere there was some truth to all this. Buddy Brown was drunk, but he was also in a panic of fear.

"You weren't scared when we walked into the Zoo and found

you with Wild."

"I didn't recognize him for a second. Then I bluffed. But I've been scared ever since. Scared all the way."

"We'll get some coffee. You need it." I wanted to know what Buddy Brown had to say.

We walked a block. Brown was silent now, still holding to my jacket sleeve. We went into a small cafe with deep booths, and I ordered a couple of coffees.

"Now what's the deal?" I asked him when the waitress turned away.

He looked down at his cup and then raised his head slowly, looking beyond me.

"I was hunted once, when I was a kid in New York," he said. I waited.

"That was ten years ago. I was fifteen then." He sounded almost sober now, his whispering voice slurred some of the words, but what he was talking about was so real to him that his drunkenness slipped away from him like a heavy, smothering cloak that he had pushed back for a little while.

"Three of us caught the girl at the edge of Central Park. She was with another girl, but we just wanted the one because her guy was the wheel with a big gang down the street. We held her skirt up over her arms and head so she couldn't do nothing but yell, and then we beat her up a little and ran away. We were all laughing when we did it because we were high on sticks, but after a while the sticks wore off.

"We were just punks. We didn't have any loot and we all lived with our folks. Next day we were afraid to go to school or be seen on the street. We knew what was going to happen. The wheel and his gang got Lee—that was one of my friends— at his house. They gave him the business while his old lady was there and his kid brothers and all. They left him alive and that was all they left him. I don't know what happened to him after that, maybe he died. He had nothing left, nothing. You know?"

He looked across the booth at me, his bruised, pale face a little twisted.

"Mick and me, we run off from home. The boys came to my house and worked over my old man to tell where I was. He didn't know, so they gave him the big schlammin. He's never going to get over it. They caught Mick downtown somewhere and they took him out on Long Island, tied him up with wire, and burned him. You know, with gasoline. He was a very sharp kid, good dancer, lot of laughs when he was high on sticks. He got burned up."

The slender, drunken boy was talking in his soft whisper, his eyes far away from mine, talking with a clear earnestness as if he were living it all again.

"I've never forgotten that year. I hid down near the produce market, sleeping in the daytime, going out at night to scrounge rotten fruit and stuff. The big rats would be out at night and I'd carry a stick and a sack of rocks. For two months I hid like that. Then it cleared up. The wheel got sent up for armed robbery and the other guys forgot about it. But I remember that year."

He drank his coffee and looked away, beyond the little cafe in Carmel-by-the-Sea.

"You want to know what happened after that?"

"I'm listening."

"My old man was sick from the beating. He worked in the shipping room at Macy's but after it happened he couldn't work there any more. The family went on relief and they wanted me to work. They got me a job at Macy's, like my old man.

"What kind of clothes can you buy on a deal like that? What can you do at night except hang around the corner and wish you had a buck? What kind of broads can you make out with? So you know what I did? I left them and went out hustling.

"What can I hustle? Who do I know? Nothing and nobody. I went back to the school where I used to go and where I knew the kids, and I hustled sticks—you know, the weed. I made enough bucks for clothes and stuff. It was a big school, maybe five-six thousand kids. Nothing great, but at least I didn't look like a jerk in cheap clothes. I found out if you live right and go along with the big men, you make out good. I never got picked up, I never had any trouble. But I'm eating my heart out all the time. Six years on the hustle and I'm nobody. I live in a hotel on Forty-ninth, I dress fine, I know a million dumb broads, I get to know a little about music and modern stuff, the big acts in show business, good cars, things like that. But I'm nobody.

"I get some real fine-looking broad with class, maybe, and I take her to the Copa. The big men are there and some of them know me. Sure, they know me as a punk hustler doing a two-bit business in weed and they wouldn't even say hello to a punk like me. I don't have it and I know it.

"So I go out to the Coast. L. A. A village, believe me, a village. New York people stand out like diamonds in L. A. I hustle. A million guys are selling weed in Hollywood and it's starvation so I do other things. Girls, mostly. A month ago I make a little score and I'm sick of L. A. so I came up here where I can be with nice people.

"I know how to talk to nice people, I dress right, I drive a right car. Nobody figures me for a punk until you come along and say it. I was going to kill you. Do you know I was going to push you around all night and then maybe kill you? I was going to find out why you fingered me to Red Kearny and what the score was and then work you over like no guy was ever worked over before. That's what I was going to do."

The thick cloak of drunkenness was slipping over him again. The whisper was louder now and he waved his hands while he talked.

"You walked away from me back in that bar. I waited outside and then it struck me. That was Broadway Red Kearny's girl that I'd been making out with, and Kearny would find out who I was—a punk, like you said, a punk. Do you think Kearny's going to let a hustler, a guy who peddles weed to school kids, make out with his daughter? It was like when I was fifteen again, only Kearny isn't just a wheel from a tough gang down the block, he's Red Kearny, and he can find me no matter where I hide. Do you understand, boy?" He half stood up on the other side of the narrow booth. "It's like when I was fifteen again—only worse. Do you understand?" He wasn't wrong. Kearny would kill him if he knew the truth. If he knew the truth, he'd find him no matter where the lean, evil boy hid.

That soft-spoken man I'd met tonight loved his daughter, and he knew the slime of the night world. He wouldn't live with himself until he'd cleansed his daughter by killing the man who had dared bring the slime to her.

Buddy was quieter now. "I didn't know who she was. I was at the Mission Ranch alone. She was dancing, sitting at the bar. I asked her for a dance. They always say yes when I ask them for a dance. I made out like a jet plane with the girl. It was just some more of this top-drawer stuff out here, as far as I knew."

He lit a cigarette, stubbed it out a moment later.

"This Brooks thing. She knows what's with Wild and me, she knows Wild is on the big beat for me. This makes it nothing but easy. Right in front of everybody, when her guy is pouring the drinks and playing the records, I ask her with the smile and the eyes. Bango! She comes whispering the time and the place to me. It was something brand-new to her, too."

He laughed. "They're pigs. All of them. Remember that and you'll make out every time. And then you'll hate them too, buster, you'll hate them."

His eyes were glittering, and he was almost sober again. He lived in a flame of intensity, and alcohol hit him fast, but burned away almost as quickly.

"Forget it," he said, standing up. "Buddy Brown's not afraid of anybody. If you see the old slob, tell him that. Tell him I'm no punk. Understand? I'm no punk."

He walked toward the door. There was somebody waiting for him there. A big man, not so big as Kearny. Brown must have seen the man, and the man must have first noticed Brown in the booth of the bright cafe.

I got up and paid the check. By now the two were together outside the door.

"Looking for you all over town. What gives?" the stranger was saying. He had immensely wide shoulders. He seemed in his middle fifties, with thick white curly hair.

Brown looked down at the powerfully built man. "It isn't all here, Sandodera. I wouldn't cross you, you know that."

"Yeah, sure, I know." Sandodera chuckled. "All your life you cross people. You crossed your own mother. You know how? By being born."

His laugh sounded jovial until you saw his eyes.

Brown noticed me in the door. "Let's get away from here. The place is crawling with crum-bum squares."

Sandodera sent one quick look at me.

"You just stumbled into the deal back there, buster, and you've taken some pushing. You don't belong with the sharp people. Come on, Joe." Brown had spoken to me, then taken the heavy man by his thick arm.

I watched them walk into the darkness.

This time I was able to find the Zoo in the lacing of dark hill streets. I was going back there because of what Buddy had said: "You just stumbled into the deal." He was right, I didn't belong in the deal. I wasn't a hard, smart guy who could work for Broadway Red, I wasn't a guy with three generations of rich family and all the right stuff like Pete and the others, I wasn't a guy who could make out with Wild Kearny the night he met her. I had the feeling of the other dimension again; I had stumbled into a world where I didn't belong. It was brighter, with blacker shadows, it was brittle and filled with a music I could almost understand. But I didn't belong there, and unless I hung on I'd wake up in my motel room tomorrow out of it forever.

I might see these people on the streets, in bars, but I couldn't get back in their world again. And that was the world where the girl I loved lived. So I drove back to the Zoo.

The Jag was there, the Nash-Healey was gone. I walked along the path through the bushes, went down the three stone steps, and pushed open the door.

Pete Barrow was sitting on one of the soft chairs in front of the fire. When he saw me he didn't stand up, but he waved the hand that wasn't holding the tall drink.

"I'm sorry," he said. He reached to the leather golf bag and pulled out a driver.

I walked over to him. He looked up and I could see that my being there wasn't important to him. For a moment I'd thought the driver was trouble, but it wasn't.

"I was kind of nasty myself," I said.

"Forget it. Everybody fights like that now. I had it coming, swinging at you before I knew the score." He fiddled with the golf club, nervous.

"Do you know the score now?" I asked.

"Yes, I think I do." He took a long drink. "Pen had a big scene with me after our hassle. Funny, I didn't know the girl at all." He dropped the club to the floor. "Sometimes I think my mother is the only person in the world I understand. But, of course, none of this is really your business, is it?"

"No."

"Just the same, do you know what the girl I was going to marry wants to do? She wants to move in with Brown. Very simple. No problems. Can you understand that?"

"A little."

"She called Wild's father and told him about his daughter. She wanted to get Wild out of the picture. Quite a girl, my once-intended bride."

We looked away from each other.

"Is Wild here?" I asked.

"In the bedroom with Pen. Just walk in."

I went to the bedroom door, pushed it open.

Pen was in pajamas, sitting on one of the two narrow beds in the small room. Wild was standing next to her. She was in her slip.

"Jim! It's all right. Come in."

There are moments in a man's living—Well, this was one of them. I walked into the room and nothing was easy for me to do, right then. Not even breathe.

Chapter Eight

I closed the door behind me. Pen was looking at the floor, Wild and I were looking at each other.

Her body was supple, smooth-limbed, small-waisted.

Her face was friendly, but she didn't smile. "Pen and I've been trying to get straight. It hasn't been working out."

She stepped across the room, picked up a cigarette and her lighter.

"Why don't you two go somewhere and leave me alone?" Pen said. Her face was tight and sullen.

Wild sat on the bed, crossed her long, golden legs. "Why did you come here, Jim?"

"I wanted to see you." I guess I smiled, because she did.

"And now?"

"We did pretty well together for a little while this afternoon. Want to try some more of it?"

"I've got to do something. It hasn't been the finest day in the world for me."

"Go out with this peasant. He's your kind—not Buddy." Pen's voice was as empty as her words.

It flooded through me with bitterness that I was standing there listening to two of Buddy Brown's women talk about him, and one of his women was the girl I'd fallen in love with.

"It's female stuff, Jim. I've been trying to tell her that jealousy is self-hate. I'm not jealous of her because I don't really hate myself. If I did, I'd be a biting, scratching wildcat of jealousy."

Pen looked at her with pure venom. "What's one man to you? Right now you're showing yourself off to another one."

Wild still sat on the bed. "One man can be important to me, Pen. There haven't been many important men to me. But believe me, I know him. I know what he is inside. It's not good. It's rotten."

"So what?" said Pen. "You're still crazy for him!"

Wild snuffed out her cigarette in a tray on a night stand. "Let's not talk any more, Pen."

I was blazing angry. "I'll tell you what I'll do. I'll take you around in my car until we find lover-boy and you can have him, and he can have you, and the hell with you both."

Pen laughed.

"I'm sorry, Jim," said Wild. I knew she meant it.

She stood up, took a wheat-yellow linen dress from a closet, and pulled it over her head. Then she ran a comb through the bronze-gold hair.

"Let's go." She stood there, regal, lovely.

We went into the big room with the soft chairs and the fireplace. Pete was still there, another drink in his hand, a George Shearing disc on the player. He'd been fooling with the Rolleiflex camera this time; it was on the floor.

"She could use a little friendship, Pete," Wild said.

"So could I. But not hers. See you around town later. Ranch, maybe?"

"Maybe. 'By."

"'By, Wild."

We walked out into the bright purple night.

"Tough for the guy," I said.

"Not so tough. He's been trying out all the lonely women at the Ranch and the Blue Ox." Wild slid into the right front seat of my Ford.

"That doesn't figure, does it?" I asked, getting behind the wheel and starting the car.

"He's a little bit afraid that he's gay—or maybe he's afraid that people will find out that he is. I don't know."

"Aren't there any nice, ordinary people in your crowd?"

She only said, "We're all off the road somewhere."

My anger and jealousy were gone. I wanted to be with her, forget the crazy Saturday, forget everything and everybody except her.

"Your father took your car?"

"He drove back to the airport to get his luggage. He'll stay at the Pine Inn."

"Then what happens?"

"He thinks his daughter is sort of stupid, sort of cheap. I don't know what happens. I know that I agree with him."

"You mean you're a woman again—you belong to yourself and not to Buddy Brown?" I turned to look at her.

She was watching the road ahead, her chin high, her full lips open. There were seconds, and I had to look back at the road. Then she spoke.

"I'm his. I don't know why. Women are like that sometimes."

I kept driving.

"Why talk, Jim? How can you talk about a man with only words to use? Words like 'rat' and 'punk' and dirtier words than those. I know all that, you know it, Red knows it.

"I know where Buddy belongs. In a bottle of gin or a half-smoked stick. With a bitter woman who hates him but who can't leave him."

I could see the picture her words made. It had reality.

"Or maybe in a cell in San Quentia. Or dead. Jim, I know, believe me, I know. But a woman doesn't live by what she knows."

It had to be said. "What about Pen Brooks?"

Her laugh was quick, scornful. "Forget it, Jim. You're a nice boy, but you don't understand this sort of thing. Pen was easy for him. Most women are. I was. Let it go at that."

Ahead was the long hill road and beyond were the lights of Monterey. I knew what I wanted for this night. Noise, and the riff of jukebox music. Drinks and darkness. This girl.

"I'm going to take you out to one of the joints near Ord. I'm forgetting everything else, Wild. A Saturday-night date in a juke joint. O.K.?"

"O.K."

We swung toward the neon fires of Seaside. I wanted to be in Seaside with Wild Kearny, in a brawling juke joint where the air would be thick with the smell of whisky and the clatter of voices with the rasp of Oklahoma or the high softness of Tennessee and Texas. Some soldier hangout where the juke would be loud and bright, spinning Rosemary Clooney or Frankie Laine, the kind of place with the kind of people I knew best and liked best.

There was the right kind of place on the side of the road and I swung into the jammed parking lot. Two soldiers were fighting near the entrance, two girls were screaming at them, and the MP's would be along in a minute to take care of them.

We found a booth inside and I ordered a couple of 7-and-7's because that was the wine of the country. The waitress was hot, sweating, and happy, pushing a wisp of too blonde hair back from her forehead, her head turned to shout something at two fat first sergeants in the next booth. I felt relaxed and easy for the first time this day.

Wild and I could find each other fast when we were alone together. I felt like a guy with his girl, the one he's been going with a for a year, the one he's going to marry in June. She had that warm, knowing closeness for me when we were together.

I guessed how she felt, too. Jim Work, O.K. and fun to be with, maybe the kind of man she could fall in love with, slowly, if she wasn't Wild Kearny. That was the bitter taste at the back of the drink, the other rhythm, strange and faraway, that you could hear behind the music.

Enough 7-and-7 highballs might wash knowing how she felt away. I was going to try it.

It was almost two and both of us were high and happy and her hand was warm in mine as we walked out to the car. We drove back on the highway toward Monterey and the motel signs were dancing in golden and scarlet neon.

"Stay with me tonight, Wild." I was watching the road ahead and my fingers were easy on the wheel.

"No, Jim. We're not like that."

"We were when we were dancing."

"I know. But I don't sleep around. I never have."

"What do we do tonight? Say good-by?"

"Probably. I don't have anything for you, Jim. Maybe I wish I had, but I don't."

She had everything any woman could ever have for me. She was mine, this girl. If I lost her I'd never be a complete man again; I'd have no pride in my maleness.

I swung the car to the right on the rutted road over the dune, toward the surge of the waters of the bay.

It was a finding without a knowing. There had been a typhoon in Tokyo once when the wood-and-paper buildings ripped before the fury. This was a typhoon between two people—a man and a woman who thought she belonged to another man.

Then it was a knowing as enemies who were once friends might know each other.

After that it was a silence between two people who should

not have been silent. We both knew now, we understood each other. We should not have been silent in that way. At last I held her in my arms again, and there was no storm, but there were no words.

She lit a cigarette, and the flame of her lighter was bright on the face of the most beautiful woman I would ever know.

"Take me home, Jim."

I backed the car over the dune, turned, and drove into the quietness of sleeping Monterey. We went along the night roads and came to the driveway beside the little house in Carmel that Wild had called the Zoo.

"Thanks for not talking. There was nothing I could have said, Jim."

She opened the door and was outside the car. I was out and we stood there together. I brought her to me, but she was not with me. A tall girl in my arms, a lovely girl, a girl behind a frozen wall, a girl who did not speak.

Wild stood there after I put my arms down, and then there was a kiss, and we were close and warm there in the darkness, kissing as lovers do when the good-by could be forever. Perhaps Wild thought it would be.

It was over, still without words, and she went down the steps and pushed open the door. There was a rectangle of soft light just before the door closed behind her.

I was halfway in the car when I heard the scream.

The Zoo door wasn't locked. I pushed it open. The big room was empty but the bedroom door was open and that room was bright with light.

Buddy Brown was there, standing, looking at Wild. She was kneeling by Pen Brooks, and Pen was sprawled on the floor, her pajama jacket pushed up, her bare stomach streaked by a stream of blood. Wild held the scissors, the blood-covered scissors.

She looked up and saw me in the doorway.

Our eyes met. She shook her head slowly and threw the scissors to the floor.

Chapter Nine

The important thing to do was to take care of the wounded girl. I went to her, bent over, and carefully, gently, quickly touched her skin above and below the wound. There was too much blood coming from it; the girl would die if she was not already dead. It's hard to tell sometimes.

Pen's lung had been cut. That's the way it looked. Her eyes were closed.

"Clean cloth," I said. Buddy stood above me, looking down at the girl.

"Let her die." His voice was thick.

"Here," said Wild. She handed me a stack of clean linen handkerchiefs.

I made a pad, pressed it against the wound.

"Call a doctor, then call the cops. The doctor first."

"Is she alive?" Wild spoke in a thin whisper.

"Get the doctor!" She saw my face, angry, intent, without patience for any wasted second.

Wild turned and Buddy grabbed her arm. Whatever rage had brought him to stab Pen was still in him.

"You stay here. I'll handle this!"

She pushed at him, tried to break away from him. He brought the heel of his hand up hard and fast against her chin and her head snapped back.

Pen's blood was flowing from around the pad. I straightened up and Buddy turned to face me. I hit him, a short left to his breastbone with my weight behind it. His mouth opened as if his face had been torn in two.

Wild had fallen backward when his fingers freed her arm. I saw her hit against the bedroom wall, slump to her knees. I stepped close to Buddy and tried with a right that was coming up with my whole body lifting it but he buried his chin against his right shoulder and I felt his thumbs jab into the arteries of my neck.

You didn't have many seconds when the carotid arteries are stopped. You feel pain, but that's a little thing; the big thing is the panic that explodes through your body when your life arteries are bursting against the relentless dams. Not many seconds—but you're taught in the dust of a sunny afternoon in basic training what you must do in those seconds before the death panic turns your muscles to slop. Arms up in front of your face and out, as if you were diving into fast water.

The terrible thumbs were shoved away.

Both of us tried the knee at the same time, but I was the one who hooked my foot under his and threw him backward. In his second off balance I got him in the breastbone again, and over the liver with the strongest punch I will ever throw in my life.

His thin, snake-like body couldn't take it. I knocked him against the wall and he tried for my eyes with his thumbs as I came into him. This time the stiff hooked-arm right coming up got him on the side of his jaw. His head banged against the wall and my hand felt as if all the fingers were broken.

He wasn't out, but he was hurt. I was seeing a funny thing —the wooden tabletop at the Mission Inn with the circles of moisture on it, the way I had seen it hours ago when I was helpless with my throat paralyzed. He got the knee this time the way the pictures in the hand-to-hand combat training manuals show, which is the same way you learn on the streets of Chicago. As he slumped I caught his hair and pulled his head back and the hard ridge of the side of my left hand hit his throat like a thick, dull cleaver. I let go and he went all the way down, face to the floor.

I stood there, and all I had left now was a heart like a bass drum and lungs that were trying to push my ribs apart. Then I bent over Pen Brooks again. She was still bleeding around the pad. I did what I could for her, but my hands were shaking and my lungs still felt hot, dry, and empty. I looked around. Where was Wild?

Just then she came back into the room and knelt next to me and Pen.

"I called a doctor. He'll be here in a couple of minutes. How is she?"

I tried to speak but my lungs weren't ready for it yet. I shook my head.

Then our eyes found each other.

I remembered the man, a little guy, a kind of Mongolian pony of a man in a dirty quilted uniform. He was looking at me as he died, his hands pressing into the torn wetness of his belly. There was hate in his eyes, and fear. There was a look as if he had a big question to ask, but mostly it was pain and hate. That was the way Wild Kearny was looking at me now. Pain, fear, hate, a big, bewildered question of some kind.

What she saw in my eyes I don't know.

We both looked away. There was too much, now, between us, too much that we had shared in passion and defeat.

"Is there anything we can do for her?"

"Wait for the doctor. Keep the blood inside of her." I could talk again, husky and gasping.

She turned her head and saw her man trying to push himself up from the floor. That was the way I thought of it, "her man." She watched him as if he were very far away.

He did it slowly, getting one knee up, resting his arm on that knee. I kept pressing the bloody pad to Pen's body. Wild stood.

"Did you call the cops?" I asked her.

Brown put one hand to the wall, leaned against it as he straightened his body.

"I called my father."

"Better call the cops."

Brown walked slowly, like a man made of wooden sticks tied together with rubber bands, one hand against the bedroom wall. He walked to the doorway, stood there a long second, and then lurched out of the room.

Wild watched him, her head turning slowly as he moved.

"Why did he do it?" I asked her.

"Goddamn life," she said, her lips tight and bitter. "Damn life, damn life to hell!"

"Wild..." My hand kept the pad firmly on the wound, but I wanted to be standing, holding Wild Kearny, telling her that she was loved, loved completely.

I had beaten the other man. I did not have to be ashamed. I had taken my woman by strength, I had broken the other man by strength. Now was the time to be gentle.

But instead I held the bloody cloth pressed tight and said only "Wild..."

"But it's no use damning life," Wild said, her voice low and clear. "Life damns you."

She opened a drawer, took out a stack of small, soft towels.

"Here. The doctor's hurrying. What else, Jim? Boiling water? Anything?"

"Boil some water. Maybe he'll want some. What is—" I couldn't say the name. "What's that punk doing?"

"I don't know. I don't think I care, either."

Pen moved, her mouth hanging open. I held my wrist watch in front of it. The glass misted slowly.

"I'll get the water boiling," Wild said.

I changed towels and watched the dying girl. All I could do for her was hold a pad against the wound.

Minutes later Wild came back.

"How is she?"

"Still alive."

"He should be here now."

"Maybe he can save her. What happened here tonight, Wild?"

She shook her head. "I came in. He was standing there, she was on the floor. The scissors were still—"

We two, who might have so much together, still were half enemies, half lovers.

"I wish I could cry for her. I can't."

"Because of Brown?"

Her lips curled. "No. I never felt any jealousy, I never hated her. I don't see why she had to be killed. I don't understand it."

"But you're not sorry for her?"

Wild shook her head. "I'm sorry that any woman can destroy herself, but I can't pity the woman, I can't weep for her. If we destroy ourselves, no one should weep, least of all ourselves."

I didn't quite understand. "Do you think she stabbed herself?"

"No. Pen wouldn't."

"The punk?"

"I don't know why he did it. He's got a wicked temper. I know."

There was something strange, distant in her voice. It was the voice of a woman who could look at herself, with passion gone. Look at herself without pity, but with a shamed knowing that somewhere still inside her she longed for the cruelty, the madness that would not be again. I felt it, and tried not to know what I felt.

We didn't hear the doctor's car but we heard his voice. Wild went to the front door. I heard his footsteps, and then I saw him, a square-faced, square-built man in a gray suit. His eyebrows were thick and white. He had his case open by the time he reached her. He lifted the bloody pack, snapped on his stethoscope, and without removing the earpieces, prepared a hypodermic, swabbed her skin, and gave her an injection.

"She's barely alive. Have you notified the police?" His eyes were cold.

"Not yet."

"Afraid to?"

"I didn't stab this girl."

"Call the police." He had gone back to work on her, his stubby fingers setting a sponge in the wound.

"O.K." I started for the big room.

"Don't try to run away."

"I won't."

Wild stood near the fireplace. As I looked at her I realized that the whisky of the night was still hot in my blood and my brain. I realized that for hours now I must have been drunk. What had happened in the car, the fight with Brown, all of this was misty now. I had been drunk, with the kind of drunkenness that lets you look all right and talk all right, while the madness stays hidden inside.

"Got to call the cops." Now my voice was sounding thick.

"Is she alive? What did he say?" Wild asked.

"He said she's barely alive. He told me to call the cops."

"My father will be here. He'll handle all that. He knows how." It was strange, the mixture of pride and bitterness in her voice on the last words.

"I'm here. I'll handle it."

I went to the phone, dialed the operator. As I waited I remembered Brown.

"Where's Brown?"

Wild shook her head. I put the phone back on the cradle just as the operator answered.

"Is he trying to get away?"

"I don't know. I'm awfully tired." As she spoke she dropped her arms to her sides and fell straight forward to the floor. That's the way men fall in a Fourth of July review on the parade ground when the sun has baked their brains—straight forward like a tree toppling. You don't fake it.

I was there beside her, lifting her head, talking to her. I don't know what I was saying, maybe telling her I loved her, maybe angry with her for passing out. I don't know. The whisky I had drunk was with me now, swirling through my eyes and my mind.

There were rapid footsteps behind me and square, stubby fingers grabbed my neck.

"What are you doing?"

"She fell over."

The doctor pushed me away. I was shaky. Then I saw the golf club on the floor where Pete or somebody had left it. When Wild had fallen she had fallen right on the club. I went in closer. The doctor was putting his stubby fingers gently on a great, swelling bruise close to Wild's temple.

He lowered Wild's head to the floor, got up slowly, warily. He didn't say anything to me but he walked quickly toward the phone, his head turning so that he could watch me as he moved.

He lifted the phone, his finger spinning the dial.

"Operator! Get the police to a small house..." His voice was muffled as he brought the mouthpiece to his lips, but his eyes never left me.

I knew what he thought: that I had hit Wild with the golf club. I was a dangerous murdering maniac. It didn't bother me. I could explain as soon as he hung up the phone. Wild would be conscious again in a minute or two.

"Wild!"

It was Broadway Red Kearny, coming through the door, across the long room to where his daughter was crumpled on the floor.

As I had done, he lifted her head, spoke to her, and then he looked at me.

"What's happened, boy? Is she hurt bad?"

The doctor answered first. "This man just clubbed her after stabbing another girl. Who are you?"

Broadway Red Kearny came up like a great bear.

"You did this?"

"No!"

"He did it just a minute ago. I came in from the other room just after he assaulted her with that golf stick."

Kearny had killed men with his hands before. I lifted my hands and he was on me, one fist swinging toward my face like a sledge.

I suppose the police saved my life. They arrived a minute or two after Kearny, and by that time the big man had me unconscious and he was choking me to death.

Chapter Ten

When I came out of it the place was very different. It was still the big, easy room with the fireplace and the record player, the room that had fitted around the four young men, the two girls, the beer, and the music yesterday afternoon. But now it was very different. It was the scene of a crime.

They had me sitting, my head back, in one of the big chairs. The watchdog of a doctor was rubbing my throat with his blocky fingers, and there was a taste of something in my aching throat, a smell of something high in my nostrils. Some kind of stimulant, acrid and metallic. I could hear a siren, going away.

As I came back the first thing I did was look for Wild. She wasn't on the floor, and the golf club was gone, too. There were three uniformed police in the room and a couple of sleepy-looking men in ordinary clothes. Broadway Red was across the room from me in another big chair. He was looking straight at me and I looked into his ice-chip eyes for a second.

"He's all right," barked the white-haired doctor, standing away from me.

I tried to lift my hands to rub my throat myself. I discovered I was handcuffed.

"What the hell's the idea?" I croaked. I waved my arms, shackled together at the wrists.

"What's what idea, son?" asked one of the men in uniform. He was blond, heavy, and he sounded tired, annoyed, but very much interested.

"Why the cuffs? Ask Wild—she'll tell you what's been happening here. I'm not the guy—"

"Suppose you tell me what's been happening here."

"Do you want to do all that here, Clyde, or take him into the station at Monterey?" asked one of the sleepy-looking men.

"Better hear his story now," said the one they called Clyde.

"Where's Wild? Is Pen Brooks all right? I mean, is she alive?" I brought the fingers of both my hands to my throat, easing off the pain of talking.

"Just tell us what happened here."

He was close to me, in front of the chair, bending over a little. One officer stood by Kearny and I could guess why. More than anything I wanted to straighten the facts out with Broadway Red. I liked the big, tough old guy and I could see why he was looking at me out of eyes filled with murder. He didn't know the story. None of these jokers knew the story if Wild hadn't come out of it yet.

"Did you see a tall, skinny guy—real tall—around here?" I asked.

The blond officer shook his head.

"His name's Brown, Buddy Brown. He's the guy that stabbed the girl."

Clyde looked at the doctor. The doctor shook his head. "Just this fellow and the girl when I got here. Besides the victim, that is. I guess it was the girl that called me. Nobody else."

"Start at the beginning, Mac," said Clyde. He wasn't talking tough, but he wasn't friendly, and I could sense the hardness in his voice.

"Wild and I were out. We came here. She went in. I heard her scream. I ran in. Buddy Brown was in the bedroom and the girl was on the floor bleeding."

"This the girl you call Pen Brooks?"

"Yes."

"Then what happened?"

"I tried to help her—first aid. Brown and I had a fight. I worked him over. He went out of the room'. Wild called the doctor while we were fighting. When the doctor got here I came out to this room. Wild fainted—she'd had kind of a rough night—and when she fell her head hit the golf club on the floor. That's about all I know."

There was silence while each of them chewed over my story. "What do you mean, she had a rough night?" Clyde asked. That was the tough question. Across the room Kearny was watching me with a cold glitter in his blue eyes.

"We'd been drinking."

"Much?"

"Quite a bit."

"Where?"

"A place in Seaside."

"Just liquor?"

"What do you mean?"

"Marijuana? Anything like that?"

"No. Where's Wild? She wasn't hurt bad, was she? She can tell you the whole story."

"She's hurt bad enough. Was that all you meant by saying she'd had a rough night?"

The tough question again. I thought for a moment. Wild had faced the bitter problem of her father and Buddy Brown yesterday. Maybe it was a problem a lot of girls have in their lives, sometime, when they know their fathers will see the cheap, dirty truths about the guys they're nuts about. For Wild it was bigger than for most girls; Broadway Red Kearny wasn't an ordinary father, Buddy Brown was dirtier than most men.

Then the good evening we'd had. After that it was Pea Brook'» blood, and the rest of it. Half drunk, with whatever I had done or we had done together, with the painful emptiness she had caused between her father and herself, with the shock of the stabbing—it had been one hell of a rough night for any girl.

But how do you explain all this to a policeman who is waiting for you to speak up?

"How bad is she hurt?"

Clyde pursed his lips. "She's unconscious. Concussion, maybe a fractured skull. It's plenty bad, son."

"She wasn't hit," I explained. "She fainted, fell straight on her face. The club was on the floor."

"What about that, Doctor?" Clyde asked, turning to the square-faced man.

"Girls don't faint much," said the doctor. "Passing out from alcohol—that's something else. But you slump when you pass out, as if your legs turn to rubber, and you don't fall hard. The kind of injury she has looked as if he'd hit her a glancing blow with that golf stick."

"What do you say about that, son?"

"She fainted. A lot of things had happened to her today. She'd drunk a lot, and she got a big shock when she got here."

"But she waited to faint until after this fight you say you had, and all the rest of it, calling the doctor and everything?"

The doctor interrupted. "That part is logical, to be fair about it. After auto accidents, any kind of shock like that, both men and women faint sometimes, minutes later, when everything's over. But this was a big, strong, healthy girl. I don't think she'd topple over, no matter what happened."

Clyde nodded. "Thank you, Doctor. Want to change your story, son?"

"No. This fellow Brown roughed her up when she started to call a doctor, a lot of things happened to her. You better find this Brown quick. He stabbed the Brooks girl."

"Why?"

"Because he's crazy-tempered and he hates women. He's psycho."

"You been in the Army, son?"

"Yeah, just got out."

"Related to anybody around here?"

"No. I'm alone. Going to stay here and go to school."

Clyde looked a little sad. He had me sized up as a young man in bad trouble and he was a little sorry for me. He was thinking about my future in terms of San Quentin, maybe, and not Monterey Peninsula College.

"About this Buddy Brown—"

"Yes?" The other officers were grouping around Clyde now.

"He was sort of involved with this Brooks girl. They must have quarreled and he lost his temper. I beat him up. He won't be far. Very tall, thin, pale."

"You say you didn't harm either one of these girls? You didn't stab Brooks, you didn't hit the Kearny girl?"

"No, sir." The Army training hadn't left me yet.

"Son, we'll find this man Brown, all right, and we'll check into your story very carefully. But—"

"Yes?"

"I don't believe you."

"I'm telling you the truth. Look for fingerprints on those scissors, on that golf club."

"Well, son, I don't believe you. One girl dying, one girl beaten with a golf club, and nobody around but you. You're pretty drunk right now, maybe you've done things you don't even remember. You'll get a fair shake, son, but it looks like you've got yourself into big, bad trouble."

Clyde went over to one of the men in civilian clothes and they talked in low tones.

"All right, son, come on. We don't have a jail here in Carmel so we're going to take you to Monterey and hold you there until Monday on an open charge. Then, the way things look now, you'll go to the county jail in Salinas. You can call a lawyer tomorrow if you want to. And you know something, son?"

I stood up, the cuffs heavy on my wrists. I was dizzy; some from the whisky, some from Red Kearny's big hands around my throat. "What?"

"You better pray those two girls don't die."

"I want to see Wild. You can take these cuffs off, too, because I don't have to run away."

"Both girls are at the Monterey Community Hospital. You won't be seeing them, not right quick, anyway. We'll leave the cuffs on. A boy who's been drinking a lot might change his mind about running away."

"How about those fingerprints? How about Brown?"

"We'll take care of everything, son. We're real careful about things."

Broadway Red Kearny got out of his chair and walked up to me. The other men closed in around him nervously and he pushed one of them out of the way.

"You didn't harm my girl?"

"No. I love your daughter."

"You didn't know her until today."

"I was pretty sure of it before we met you at the airport. I'm dead sure now."

These were cold blue eyes that had looked into the core of many a man. There was a long searching and the others in the room were quiet and motionless.

Kearny's face was like reddish rock. "Yes. I'll back your play."

I had one man who believed me in the room, and he was the only one that mattered.

They led me out, up the three stone steps, past my Ford, and to the open rear door of a police sedan. The front seat was protected from the rear by a screen of heavy wire. Two of the uniformed officers got in back with me; one of them was Clyde. The driver got in, started the car, spoke into the radio telephone briefly, and then backed the sedan into the street.

"You were kind of lucky," said Clyde.

"Yeah," I said, "this is my lucky night. My girl's in the

hospital, I'm in jail."

"You could be at the morgue. It took three of us to pull that Kearny off you."

"He's a good man. He just got the wrong idea when he walked in."

"You always drink this much, son?"

The car was climbing the long hill now. Carmel was dark and sleeping.

"No. It wasn't an ordinary day. A lot of beer in the afternoon, some stuff at dinner, whisky at that place in Seaside. Brown was drunk, too. Earlier in the evening. He got drunk fast. He's dead scared of Kearny."

"Why?"

I didn't say anything. It wouldn't be easy to explain that the one girl in the world for me had been sleeping with a man so rotten that he was afraid her father would kill him for his rottenness. It wouldn't be easy.

"I'm not sure. Like I said, he's a psycho."

"How long have you known these people?"

"Just today, yesterday. Saturday."

"How'd you get involved?"

"There was a little car accident. We got to talking. Wild introduced me to her father. Later I went to the cottage and we went out."

"Who was there? This Brown?"

"No. Another man. Pete Barrow. He was engaged to Pen Brooks."

"But she was playing around with Brown?"

"Yes."

"And when you came back with the Kearny girl, Brown was there with Miss Brooks?"

"Yes, sir. She'd been stabbed. Brown said to let her die."

"But you tried to help her?"

"A little. I've been in Korea. Sometimes you have to help a guy until the medic can get to him."

The car whistled through the blackness between the great trees at the crest of the Carmel hill. In front the police telephone rattled in a faraway voice at intervals.

"You know how it is, son," Clyde said. "You tell a pretty straight story, I'll say that. But you didn't call the police, even after the doctor told you to. The girl may have fainted, but nobody thinks she did. Girls don't faint, not girls like that one. They'll be in there pitching when the average boy is frazzled down to his socks. You were pretty drunk tonight. There's only your word, so far, about this Brown. One girl stabbed, one girl slugged with a golf club, and you were the only person there. You understand how it is, don't you?"

"Yes, I understand how it is," I said.

Take it cool, I told myself. Kearny believes you now. He liked you from the beginning. When Wild wakes up, she can tell them the rest of the story. I spend a night in jail, so what? I've told the facts a couple of times, all the facts. All the facts except that Wild Kearny used to be Buddy Brown's girl. All the facts except that a couple of hours ago I found that she was mine, and never Brown's again.

Through the mesh of wire I could see the lights of Monterey and Seaside with the light-flecked shimmering of the bay beyond.

The police car turned off the main highway as we came into Monterey, the old part of Monterey where many of the buildings were once the homes of the great Spanish families a century and more ago.

We swung past a small park and the car pulled in behind a large building and stopped. I could see a naked electric light over a wooden door in a frame shed and another building, a low, one-story stone structure. Beneath the light was a sign, "Police and Prisoners Only." That was us. We had a ticket.

Clyde led me through the doorway.

"Got one for you," he said. "Book him open."

The man behind the desk was in uniform shirt sleeves. He yawned, scratched his head, and came over.

"Figure Carmel wants to spend the ten bucks?"

Clyde laughed. "For this one, yes. But if he asks for a blanket, be sure and lock the cell after you give it to him. He turned to me and put his key to the handcuffs. He was chuckling. I got the idea that he had begun to believe me, a little. "Carmel has to pay Monterey ten dollars a night to keep our prisoners in their jail. A while back a Carmel prisoner asked for a blanket and the lockup forgot to lock up. Prisoner just walked away."

The handcuffs fell open and away. "Carmel and Monterey are still arguing about the ten bucks," Clyde added. "We say we don't owe for a full night since they didn't have him in the morning. They just want the ten bucks. Fingerprints now, son."

They inked my fingers, one at a time, and rolled them off on a card.

"You aren't wanted someplace else for something, are you?' asked Clyde. "No."

"Might as well speak up if you are, because we'll find out about it by Monday anyway."

"What about my car? It's parked back there at that house. I wasn't much concerned or interested in the procedure of booking me. I knew that by Monday I'd be back in normal life again, normal as it could be considering that I was in love with Wild Kearny.

"Got to check over your car a little. It'll be here waiting for you if you get out. Which brings us to your keys, money, billfold, all that stuff. Get everything out of your pockets and put it in this envelope."

I emptied my pockets. The man in shirt sleeves sealed the envelope. He took out another card and had me spell my name, my address, my Army history, previous addresses, the whole works.

"We're going to run lab tests on his clothes," Clyde told the desk officer.

"O.K. there, fellow. Start taking your duds off." He went into a back room while Clyde watched me. The officer came back, tossed me a faded denim shirt and a pair of patched denim pants. I put them on.

"How about my belt? These damn things are ten sizes too big." I pulled them out from my flat stomach. "No belt. How do you get along with fleas?"

"No good. They like to chew the hell out of me."

"You going to have a scratchin' good time tonight, then, bub."

They led me into the one-storied stone building next door. The old prison had smells stacked up on each other. Sour smells of ancient sin, dirty smells from Saturday-night drunks, acid smells from disinfectants.

A heavy key creaked in a heavy lock and a heavy door was

pulled open and shut behind me. The key creaked again. I was in jail. The first flea bit me and I began to scratch.

It looked like a bad night, the hour or so that was left of it. "Hey! You sober?"

I could see a head peering down at me from the upper bunk. The cell was big enough for one double bunk. "Yeah, I'm sober. Pretty much."

"Good. Was figuring it was just about time for them to put a hootin' and hollerin' drunk in here, being Saturday night and all." I could see the face a little now. It looked like a pixie out of Walt Disney in the bad light.

"What are you in for, pardner?" The voice sounded young, and it had a twang that was maybe Texas or Oklahoma.

"Nothing. They got me mixed up with another guy."

"Good boy! I like being in with an old-timer. You always learn something."

"No, seriously. On the level. It's just a little mix-up."

"That's my pardner talking like I like to hear him talk. What's your name?"

"Jim Work. No kidding, fellow, it was another guy. I'll be out tomorrow."

"My name's Dooley. Billy Dooley. Glad to meet you."

"Here, too. These fleas bother you?" I was scratching energetically now.

"Fleas? Pardner, a couple years ago when I first hit the road the fleas ate all the meat off my bones. When a flea climbs my frame now he just slides off disgusted-like."

I sat down on the bunk. Right now I felt pretty damn miserable. There was the liquor wearing off, and my sore throat and general aches all over. But it was mostly Wild being in the hospital. I wanted to be with her, to wash the hate and bitterness out of her clear eyes.

"What they got you in for, Dooley?" Might as well talk. The night was terrible in its loneliness.

"Curiosity, mostly. This part of the country is running wild with sports cars. They've got MG's for the peasants, and they've got Jags like Oklahoma has rabbits. I kind of tried out a Jag for size, a little. Weren't mine."

I stretched out on the bunk.

"I'm a magician," Dooley said. "That's my trade. Miracles

and stuff."

"What do you mean, miracles?"

"You know, like a magician does. Things you can't believe that you see right in front of your eyes 'cause I make 'em happen. The unbelievable, the impossible."

It was a strange conversation in the solitude of the cell, yellow-lit from a dim bulb. Outside was the quiet of the night, nearby the jailer was probably sleeping, a few miles away two girls were in hospital beds. Somewhere in the outer darkness was a lean, hard-muscled, hot-eyed man named Buddy Brown.

"Where do you do your magic?"

"Anyplace. Taverns and cocktail lounges. Sometimes schools. Wherever I am and there's an audience. Freest man in the world, pardner, that's Dooley the Fantastic."

"Not now, you aren't."

Dooley laughed.

"Where are you from?" I asked.

"Tulsa, Bartlesville, Rincon. Places like that. I move along, mostly."

"Why did you steal the Jaguar?"

"I'd never driven a Jag, and it didn't look like I was saving money fast enough to buy one real soon. I was just samplin' it, kind of."

"How'd the cops catch you?"

"I guess maybe I didn't look like the Jag type. Just going by in a police car and they looked at me, and then they looked a little more, and then they said, 'Hey, you, pull over.' Didn't sound like they figured a li'l ol' country boy like me belonged in it. Didn't have a report on the car or nothing. 'Bout an hour ago or so. I think I'll try to grow a mustache. Might help."

I didn't answer and we both were quiet. In a little while I heard Dooley snoring gently. He sounded like a nice kid.

Chapter Eleven

The night the loneliness engulfed me. I thought of Buddy Brown.

They'd find him somewhere tonight. Walking on a dark street between the hills. In his bed. Sitting alone in his room with a bottle. Sitting alone and laughing, with the brown cigarette cupped in his hand, the weed-sweet smell thick in the room. Maybe now an officer, hand on his holstered gun, was walking toward Buddy Brown in the lonely Greyhound waiting room at Salinas while the heavy-eyed soldiers and huddled Mexicans watched. Maybe a state highway patrol car was flagging down the MG on 101. Night thoughts. Night thoughts on a bunk, scratching flea bites.

They wouldn't find him. It was a night truth, one of those things that you know as you lie awake toward dawn. Maybe they'd look for him, but they wouldn't find him.

I moved restlessly on the sagging bunk.

If Pen Brooks died, only two people would know who killed her. Wild Kearny was one, and I was the other. If Wild Kearny died...

Night thoughts. If a snake whip of a man went to Wild's hospital bed tonight in the darkness, a man who would know the simple trick of killing an unconscious person without leaving marks or traces—the simple trick of the soft pressure through folded cloth on the carotid arteries until the brain died, blood-starved—then it would be Jim Work that would inhale the gas in that little room in the big house above San Francisco Bay. There were no other witnesses against Brown.

Wild was in danger. That was the alarm bell that exploded through the night thoughts. I swung out of bed, pounded on the heavy door.

"What's the trouble, pardner? Want a better room? I don't figure they have any."

I didn't answer Dooley. I kept pounding on the door.

"Hey you, you crazy or something?" The jailer's voice was gruff, complaining. He came up to the heavy door.

"I've got to talk to the Carmel police. It's a matter of life and death."

"Get back in your bunk. You're going to see plenty of police tomorrow."

"Then call the hospital. Tell them to put a guard on Wild Kearny."

"Why should they? We got you in here."

Clyde must have told him the story after they'd locked me away.

"This fellow Brown. If he kills her, he can beat this."

"Get back in your bunk." He walked away.

I pounded on the door until my bruised hand was hot with pain. He didn't come back.

I tried to think. Brown wouldn't know what had happened. He wouldn't know that I had been arrested for the stabbing of Pen Brooks. He wouldn't know that Wild Kearny was unconscious or in the hospital. I pushed the night thoughts back into the shadows. I'd blown my top.

But the night thoughts returned insistently.

Brown wouldn't know yet what had happened, but he would think as I did when he learned the whole story, and his plans would be more subtle, more dangerous. He would act for reasons of which I knew nothing.

Even as the deep fear for Wild circled through my head and the fear for myself, I slid into sleep while the January dawn moved across the hills in the east.

I was jerked out of it by the jailer's voice.

"Chow time. Wash up."

Billy Dooley slid down from his bunk. In the morning light he had the face of a freckled Irish pixie out of Oklahoma, and eyes laughing as if he were just about to push the outhouse over behind the school with the teacher inside it.

"Hi, pardner. Wanna see some magic?"

They hadn't taken Dooley's clothes. He wore almost skintight jeans, a red and white checked shirt, a green bow tie, and scuffed, high-heeled cowboy boots.

Before I answered Dooley waved his hands, passed one over the other, and there was a rose in his palm. It was a paper rose, and a little beat up. His hands moved and he was holding an egg, a rubber egg with a Scotch-tape patch on it. He clapped his hands, there was a little bright flash, a puff of smoke and the egg was gone.

"Fantastic, ain't it? Of course, it's a little more fantastic if you're kind of farther away." He was smiling like a proud but bashful kid.

"You mean they left you your magic stuff?"

He dug one boot against the other. "It's kinda hard to search a magician real good. Practically takes another magician to do it, and these John Laws aren't magicians. Except at figuring out guys that don't belong in Jags at three o'clock in the morning."

"Hey, you, we're going out for chow." The jailer was pushing the heavy key into the door. He swung it open, slapped his pistol holster in a very broad hint, and motioned us along. We washed up, and he took us out into the morning brightness of Monterey.

He took us across the street and around the block to a pleasant little cafe. We had a stack of wheat cakes and a cup of coffee apiece. It tasted fine, in spite of a hangover and plenty of bruises that bounced around my body.

"How about a phone call?" I asked the jailer. He was a fat man with a good-natured face, not the one who had booked me the night before.

"Who you going to call?"

"I want to call the Community Hospital."

"'Bout them girls you beat up?"

"Make it easy on both of us," I said to the jailer. "I don't know what the night man told you, but I'm being held on an open charge. I didn't beat up or hurt any girls, and if Wild Kearny is conscious I'll be out of your flea circus in an hour. How about calling?"

"You got any money in your envelope?"

"Enough."

His eyes narrowed and his good-natured face clouded up. "I didn't mean that. If you got a dime for the phone, that's all you need. I'll loan it to you now. Use that phone booth, and I'm lettin' you in there with this dime to call your lawyer. Understand?""I understand. Thanks." He gave me the dime and watched me go to the booth.

There was a slim phone directory in the booth. I found the hospital number and dialed it.

"Monterey Community Hospital, good morning, a woman's voice said.

"I'm calling to find out the condition of Miss Wild Kearny."

"One moment, please."

I scratched a flea bite and waited.

"Yes?" This was a nurse's voice, coolly pleasant but with plenty of conscious authority.

"How is Miss Wild Kearny, please?"

"Who is calling?"

"Jim Work."

"Are you a relative?"

"A friend." It was a funny word to use, but what else? Lover? The guy who's in the jug accused of slugging her? A friend.

"She's doing well."

"Is she conscious? Is she awake? Could I talk to her?"

"She's doing well. No visitors or phone calls."

"How about Pen Brooks?"

"We are not permitted to give any further information." She hung up.

It wasn't much of a dime's worth. I walked out of the booth and the fat man slapped his holster again and paraded us to the door. We went back to the jail and he put us back in the cell and closed the heavy door.

"Won't work you boys much, 'cause it's Sunday. Got a couple drunks in the other tank to sweep up and mop. Do 'em good." He rumbled away.

I stretched out on my bunk and went to sleep. Billy Dooley was disappointed: he'd planned to give me a magic show. He was practicing with a deck of cards as I sank into sleep.

Chapter Twelve

It was after twelve when they came for me. The jailer opened the cell door and shook me awake. This time it took a few seconds before I remembered where I was and what it was all about.

I slid out of my bunk, rubbed my eyes, and yawned. Billy was asleep in the upper bunk.

"Come on," said the jailer.

"Lunch?" I was going to wake Dooley.

He shook his head. I had the feeling things were bad.

"More important than lunch. Come on." This time he held my arm as he closed the door and locked it. For a fat man he had strong fingers.

He walked me down a corridor, up some stairs, and into a room, holding my arm tightly all the while.

"Here he is," he said to the three men in the room. Clyde, who was probably the chief in Carmel, was sitting at a table with a man in civilian clothes. A uniformed officer was standing near the door.

"Sit down," Clyde said, motioning to a chair. His voice had changed since last night. It was cold and businesslike now.

The uniformed officer closed the door and stood in front of it.

"This is Mr. Gloster from Burr Scott's office," said Clyde. "Burr Scott is the district attorney for Monterey County."

I nodded. The other man didn't nod back.

"Tell us exactly what happened last night. Start yesterday afternoon or evening. Tell it slowly and don't leave out anything." Clyde spoke carefully, coldly.

"Have you picked up Buddy Brown?" I asked.

"Just tell your story," Clyde said. He wasn't calling me "son" today.

"I'd like to know about Brown. Wild Kearny is the only witness outside of myself, and if Brown's loose she may be in danger."

Clyde shook his head. "She's in no danger from Brown. Now

tell your story." He meant it.

"It started with an accident yesterday afternoon. On Ocean Avenue in Carmel. My car turned over Brown's MG. Not much damage, nobody hurt."

Clyde nodded. "I saw the report."

"Brown and I had a little fight. One punch. His."

The D.A.'s man was making notes.

"Then we went to the home of Wild Kearny. She lived there with Pen Brooks." I went on with the story. The fight back of the house. Wild and I going to Monterey, to the airport to meet her father, leaving out the reason. The dinner at the Hearthstone. Later, the incident at the Mission Inn, Pen Brooks and Pete Barrow. Meeting Buddy Brown, drunk. What he had told me of himself. Going to the Zoo again.

"We went to a juke joint in Seaside. We drank and danced. Talked about things. Then ..." I wondered if my face showed anything, if these men could notice.

"Yes?"

"Then I drove her home. She went inside. I heard her scream and ran in." I told them the same story I had told Clyde the night before.

"That's all of it," I said.

"You're sure? Nothing left out?"

"Nothing."

"You'd swear to it?"

There was the squeeze. I'm pretty tough-minded; it's a tough world, where the best you can do is take care of yourself. But an oath is important. I didn't feel like lying under oath.

"Speak up. Will you swear to it?"

"Not right now."

I was aware of the speculative stares of both men.

"What role did you play with Miss Kearny and Miss Brooks?"

"I knew them slightly. Pen Brooks, that is. I spent several hours yesterday with Wild Kearny."

The laugh wasn't friendly. "Yeah, I'll bet you did. You meet her yesterday, last night you take her to the Corral in Seaside, and the waitress remembers you as a sweet couple. That's what she called you. She recognized a picture of the girl and described you."

"So what? Maybe we are a sweet couple."

"The Corral closes at the regular hour. Then what did you do?"

"We talked in my car."

"What did you talk about?"

"We talked about the foreign policy of the United States."

"You think being smart's going to help, kid?"

I didn't answer.

"Why didn't Miss Kearny phone the police?"

"She phoned her father."

"Did you ever talk about foreign policy with Pen Brooks?"

"No."

"How did Wild Kearny get along with the Brooks girl?"

"Fine."

"In spite of the fact that both of them were in love with Buddy Brown and possibly with you?"

Damn. I waited, silent. People's lives were never meant to be naked in the cold machinery of law. But what else is law for?

"Did Miss Kearny stab Pen Brooks?"

"No. It was Buddy Brown. If you want co-operation from me, you'll have to tell me if Brown has been caught."

I was going to have to fight. Not for myself; I didn't feel afraid or worried. I wasn't fighting to save Wild Kearny, either. I wasn't worried about their suspicions. I was fighting evil—the dirty, snakelike trail of Buddy Brown that festered into corruption behind him. I was fighting for the hope of something decent and good for Wild Kearny and Jim Work together.

"We're still looking for Brown."

"Thanks." It was a bitter word as I said it. "Is Wild conscious yet?"

"We found out why she fainted. Sometime—maybe from this Brown, as you say, or maybe from you, earlier—she received a bad blow on the back of her head. If your story is true, Miss Kearny was helping you with the Brooks girl, making her call to the doctor and all that, in intense pain, fighting off unconsciousness. She is still unconscious."

The heel of Brown's hand snapping Wild's head back, her head hitting the wall behind her. I remembered.

"We'll hold you here for arraignment tomorrow, Work. Then you'll be taken to Salinas. You are being charged with the murder of Penelope Brooks. She died this morning."

I stood up and the policeman behind me stepped forward, one hand on my arm.

"Then Brown's your murderer. Wild will tell you that."

"We don't know what Miss Kearny will tell us. There are some things we do know. You were with this girl for a long time somewhere last night. Then the two of you went to her house. Sometime later the girl calls a doctor. Then the girl is slugged. Nobody calls the police until the doctor does.

"What we want to know is this: Are you trying to cover up for the Kearny girl?"

"No."

"Just for fun, supposing this happened. Supposing you sell the Kearny girl a big line of goods yesterday. Bigger than Brown's. You go out and have fun. You come back. Brooks threatens to tell the old boy friend about the two of you. There's an argument. Maybe Kearny stabs Brooks, maybe you do.

"Then the doctor comes. You're scared. You tell the Kearny girl to help you frame Brown. She refuses. You slug her. How does that sound, fellow?"

"Lousy."

"It's lousy, all right. Damn lousy. But it happened that way, didn't it?"

"Have you found Brown?"

"He'll be picked up. We'll check out your story. But the only fingerprints on those scissors seem to be the girl's. The only people we know were there were you and the girl."

"Wild will tell you the truth."

"So you say."

"What are you holding me for right now?"

"Suspicion of murder. You'll be arraigned tomorrow. It's up to you what Burr Scott will ask for."

"How do you mean?"

"We're thinking about first-degree murder. How does that sound to you?"

"Fine."

"What do you mean, fine?" The eyes were hard, and the faces moved closer to mine.

"Find a tall, thin man with a pale face. Charge him with murder and you'll have two good witnesses."

"You for one?"

"I didn't see him stab the girl. Otherwise, yes."

"Try this one for size, fellow. Let's say Brown really was there."

"He was."

"You don't go in with the Kearny girl. She went in, found Brown and the Brooks girl—well, let's say she found them talking about American foreign policy. You know how women are, don't you, fellow?"

I kept my mouth closed, my teeth hard together.

"Sure you know how women are. You do real good the same day you meet one. The fact that she's been finding out how the night air feels with you maybe doesn't keep her from thinking that Pen Brooks should keep her hands off her other boy friend. So she stabs her. How does that sound?"

It didn't sound very good, but I didn't say anything.

"Well," Gloster said, his fingers drumming on the table, "let him stay here in storage until tomorrow morning. If things haven't changed by then we'll charge him with murder. Do you have a lawyer, Work?"

"No, and I won't need one." I was thinking about money. Fifty dollars at the least if I asked some attorney to represent me. I wasn't nervous or worried, and fifty dollars was a lot of money to me.

Gloster looked at me, shoved his lower lip over the upper one. "O.K. We'll see." He nodded to the policeman behind me.

The officer opened the door and led me back downstairs. The fat man put me in the cell.

"What's the story, pardner?" Dooley asked.

"Giving me a bad time," I said.

"Trouble?"

"Some. My girl's in the hospital unconscious. They think I slugged her and killed another girl."

Dooley's pixie eyes widened. "You don't look mean."

"I'm not." I told Dooley the whole story, everything. There are times when the best thing you can do is open up to somebody else. This was the time. I needed to say a lot of things out loud, not because of Dooley, but because when you say them to someone else they make more sense to you.

"Best this girl of yours gets well fast. Until she does, these boys are going to twist your arm good. Too bad you didn't work that Brown down a little more. Shouldn't have let him move out like that."

"I was busy with the Brooks girl. Brown didn't look as if he could walk ten feet.

"Skinny ol' boys got a lot of grit in their craws," said Billy. "Want to see some magic?"

"Go ahead, Houdini."

The kid did tricks for an hour. When he'd been booked he had sleighted a small box full of magical equipment and a sack with some more stuff. It was amazing what he could do—card tricks, ventriloquism, disappearing objects, everything. I liked it and I never asked how the tricks were done, so he knocked himself out entertaining me.

The good-natured fat man took us out to lunch and Billy bedeviled him with ventriloquism at the cafe's lunch counter. Then Billy made a puppet out of a couple of paper napkins, two spoons, and two knives. The little puppet bawled the fat man out for spilling his soup, made fun of his double chin, and flirted with the waitress.

When we got back to the jail Gloster was waiting for me. He had another man from the District Attorney's office with him. The jailer put Billy into the cell and took me back upstairs with Gloster. They closed the door.

"I've met some pretty crumby specimens in this job," Gloster said to me, "but you're the prize."

"What the hell do you mean? Is there something about working for the District Attorney that gives you a license to pop off any time you want to?" I was ready to swing at him. I knew that they'd handle me rough if I did, but I was plenty angry.

"Work," said Gloster and he spat out the words, "a reputable witness showed up at the Carmel police station at noon and explained that he'd heard about the Brooks affair on the local news broadcast. The news broadcast said that the police were searching for Buddy Brown.

"This witness is willing to swear that Brown was at his home from midnight until nearly four this morning playing records and drinking coffee. He's also willing to bring in another witness of the highest character to affirm that Brown was there during those four hours. Now what do you have to say?"

"Who is this witness?"

"You'll find out in due course. We're satisfied as to his reliability. His story knocks out not only your clumsy attempt to frame Brown, but also your dirty attempt to smear the dead girl."

"What do you mean?"

There was no doubt of Gloster's contempt for me. He didn't bother to answer me.

"Do you want to tell the truth now? All I want to know is who actually did the stabbing, this Kearny woman or you? Everything leads me to believe that she killed Miss Brooks except for your attack on her later. We're not going to bargain with either of you now. One or both of you are going to be tried for murder in the first degree. If you didn't do it, you'd better get out from under in a hurry, because there's going to be a conviction in this case and we're going to ask for death. Understand?"

"Your witness is lying," I said.

"These witnesses belong to one of the oldest and most respected families in Pebble Beach. Their testimony is unimpeachable. You can stop this pretense now, Work. The rest of it is up to you. If you did it, I guarantee you'll go to the gas chamber. If you didn't do the actual stabbing, this is your last chance."

There was no point in my talking to Gloster now. He was sure of himself, angry and contemptuous.

"Brown did it. I don't care who your witnesses are, they're lying. Either Brown has something on them or he's bought them. I want to know two things: How is Wild Kearny, and have you found Buddy Brown?" I spoke evenly, without passion.

"I'm not here to answer your questions. You'll do the answering."

"Then there's nothing to say."

"Do you want an attorney?"

"I don't need one. I'd like to talk to Mr. Kearny."

"If he wants to see you, he'll have to get permission from Mr. Scott."

"Can I call him?"

"We'll call an attorney for you. You're entitled to that, and you'll not get one damn thing from our office except the strict legal rights any prisoner has. You're facing a murder charge and you have damn few rights."

Chapter Thirteen

Even the cheerful fat man had changed when he took me back to the cell. He knew that Burr Scott's office was sure of me now, sure that I'd been involved in the nasty murder of a young woman. There was no warmth for me; he took me to the cell as if he were a mechanical man, chill and unapproachable.

Dooley was asleep.

The jailer locked the door. "I've got special instructions on you, Work," he said. "You don't go out to eat any more. I'll bring your meal to you in the cell. If you decide to call a lawyer, you're to tell me and I'll do the calling." He walked away, righteous, unemotional.

What I had in my mind were the night thoughts, the night truths again. The strength of evil. A Buddy Brown is not weak or helpless; he has secret strengths, secret dark helpers. He's not especially smart, maybe he's even a little stupid. His own life is empty and terrible. In the end, always, he will destroy himself. But while he lives, because he is evil, he has dark strengths. Everything that is weak in a decent person, every lust or abnormal desire, gives power to the Buddy Browns.

I sat on my bunk and looked at the truth. It wasn't important that Brown had found witnesses to lie for him. It wasn't even important that I was in a bad jam. The big thing was that here and now I was face to face with evil in a showdown battle.

Let's get practical, boy, I said to myself, and pushed the deeper thoughts away.

Brown knew the score now: Wild still unconscious, suspected of the stabbing, with her fingerprints on the bloody scissors; Work in jail; police hunting for Brown. Sometime on this Sunday morning he had found a way of making respected people lie for him.

Absolute safety for him still meant Wild Kearny's death. She might even know or guess the kind of pressure he had used to get his witnesses. If she lived, her father would believe her, regardless of what the law and the courts did. Believing her, he would hunt down Buddy Brown, and he would find him.

Kearny had tamed the forces of evil. He knew them and he could use them. The people of the night world would hunt Buddy Brown for Broadway Red Kearny. The weary hustlers, the worried little crooks, the whole web of the night would be spread across the continent for Buddy Brown. They would all know that Broadway Red Kearny was looking for a tall, thin pimp and reefer-pusher named Buddy Brown. Kearny would get him and that would be the end.

Broadway Red wouldn't kill him. He'd break him and turn him in, sobbing, spilling his guts in confession. I knew that. Brown would know that, too.

I tried to imagine that I was Buddy Brown.

How would I kill Wild Kearny?

It would have to be fast, before she could regain consciousness and talk. It would have to look like suicide. Wrists slashed with a razor blade, maybe. Or maybe Brown would have some other scheme, a surer one. But no matter what his scheme, he had to kill Wild Kearny, and quickly.

It wouldn't be an easy thing to do. Her father would be there, maybe in the room, and there would be either a police matron in the room or a policeman outside her door. The whole routine of the hospital would be there to protect her. No visitors except maybe her father. He'd be a hard man to get around. A girl in bed with walls around her, with guards around her, watched by nurses. It looked as if she should be safe.

But Brown had no choice. He had to find a way, and he would.

The cell around me seemed to close in on me like stone fingers. For the first time I felt imprisoned, helpless, trapped.

Brown was probably free to move. If the police had found him, they would have brought the two of us together. Now, with his alibi, they wouldn't even bother to pick him up.

Wild might still be unconscious. Tonight, maybe sooner, would try to kill her. I was in a cell, behind a heavy door.

As I had last night, I pounded on the door.

The fat man came to the grille. "What's the matter?"

"I've got to explain something."

"You do your explaining at court tomorrow morning. You don't explain nothin' to me."

Like the guard last night, he turned away.

"Let me talk to Gloster, anybody. Let me make a phone call!"

He was gone.

They wouldn't believe me, anyway. Brown had his Pebble Beach alibi. No matter how I explained things, they wouldn't believe me. I was an unknown, unimportant ex-soldier. I'd been found drunk in a house with two girls, one dying, one knocked out. I'd accused a man who had brought respected witnesses to testify that I was lying. They wouldn't believe me.

"You really like pounding on that ol' door, don't you, pardner?" said Dooley, peering down at me from his bunk.

"I've got to get out of here. Somehow I've got to get out of here."

"Sounds reasonable, pardner. This place really don't have much. Not a good neighborhood, practically no conveniences, and confining as hell. Don't much care for it myself." He slid down from the bunk. "Howsoever, here we are. Might as well make the best of it and quit bashing your hand on that door. That ol' fat man ain't fixing to come back no matter how you pound."

Helpless, trapped. It was the first time in my life that I had felt completely trapped. Nothing to fight against except the iron bars and stone walls. The hours would go by, and somewhere outside Brown would be moving toward Wild Kearny.

I had to get out of this cell. I had to go to Wild. I had to find Brown and do myself the job that Kearny would do if Wild could talk—break him, bring him to the police, confessing the truth that would destroy him.

"What you puzzling over, pardner?"

"I'm going to try to escape, Billy." I hadn't meant to tell him.

"I'm going to have to take you home and introduce you to my folks."

"Why?"

"They got the idea that I'm crazy. I want to show 'em the real thing."

I sat on my bunk, looking at the door.

"Pardner, these walls are mighty thick and those bars are mighty strong. Ol' fat man got him a big roscoe on his hip and I believe that man knows how to use it. Got shootin' eyes. You cause him trouble and he'll mess up your insides with those slugs. Maybe I'd better do some magic for you."

"Billy, I've got to talk. I've got to explain to somebody why I've got to get out of here."

I told him what I thought Brown would do. He listened carefully, shrewdly, and the pixie face was serious when I was finished.

"Believe you're right, pardner. This mean-tailed boy Brown's got it cold in front of him. If this girl talks—especially to her old man—Brown has had it. He's a gone pigeon, if he knocks the girl off, he's got a fine chance of going on his way whistling. The answer is, knock the girl off fast."

We both were on my bunk and for a little while we were silent.

"Maybe I could call this Broadway Red Kearny on the phone for you."

"See if the fat man will let you."

Billy went to the door. "Hey, what do you want me to do with all this whisky I found back here under the bunk?" he yelled.

The fat man came huffing to the door. "What whisky you talkin' about?"

"I want to phone my lawyer. How's about it, huh?"

The fat man came huffing to the door. "What whisky you—no whisky in there. No, nobody calls nobody today any more. I got my orders. Nobody calls nobody and nobody talks to nobody. Nobody." He went off, puffing a little.

"When we go out to eat—" began Billy.

"I'm not going out. I'm a bad one, so I get my meal brought to the cell."

"This cheese is sure binding, ain't it?"

"I'm going to try a break. When he brings in my food."

Billy looked at me, his face excited and happy. "Can't be an escape act with Dooley the Fantastic around unless Dooley is in it. You know that, pardner."

"Billy, there's no reason for you to break out. You'd only get in more trouble. You pretend you're asleep when I try it."

"Pardner, I'd never live it down. I'm supposed to be a magician, escape artist and all that. How would it look if an amateur like you escaped and a professional magician like me stayed cooped up? Besides, I want to get out of here before have to face that ol' judge in the morning. That ol' boy is likely to say something silly, like 'Five years.'

"They won't give you five years for borrowing a car. Probation, most likely."

"Seems I've been in a little trouble before, here and there, for this and that. If that ol' judge takes a notion, he could get real silly. Best that I leave these parts."

"No dice, Billy. You stay here."

"Pardner, I've got to go. I'm goin' to go. Curtain."

I was thinking. I had to break out, and I knew that if I did, Billy would go too.

"That key is on a big ring. What can you do about that, Billy?"

"I can get it off. Slick as chicken guts. But that won't do no good, pardner. Only time I could get it was when we were out eating, and he'd need it to open up and let me back in."

"If you're going to try to break out too, Billy, I don't want to use force. We've got to outsmart him."

"That fat man's in the jail business. Probably pretty smart about his own business. A magician generally would use misdirection of some kind, making you look there when the gimmick is being worked here. Got to make ol' fat man look where we ain't."

"When you were showing me those tricks, Billy, how did you make that bright flash of light and puff of smoke?"

"These papers. Most magicians use them." He took some thin tissues from his little box of equipment. "There's a tiny cap at one end that explodes when you hit it, then the rest of the tissue burns real quick. It's a kind of guncotton."

"Could you fix some of them so that when he opens the door, they'll go off at the hinges?"

"Easy, pardner."

"If you could get that key off the ring, maybe you could lift his gun when he wasn't looking? I mean, could you ease that gun out of his holster?"

"Love to."

"O.K., Billy. Fix those flash papers at the hinges. Then we sit tight till he comes to get you for supper. That'll be around four o'clock, maybe. The fat man's relief won't show up until maybe six. Set the papers so I'll know how to do it. Then we unset them again. He takes you over for supper, brings mine back. When he opens the door the flash will go off."

"Going to kind of surprise him."

"You try to lift his gun as soon as you get in the building, before he gets to the door."

"If he don't make me carry the tray. Having met the law socially pretty often, I'm going to guess that I carry the tray."

"In that case, we'll have to risk his having the gun. The door opens, the flash goes off, he turns to look with the key still in the lock, I pull him in, slide out, you slam and lock the door. What do you think?"

"It's simple enough. Might work."

"We'll have to run. He'll start shooting and there's a whole nest of cops next door. After that I don't know what happens."

"I'll tell you one thing that'll happen," said Billy.

"What?"

"Your pants will fall down."

I'd got used to my loose jailhouse pants, making the holding of them with one hand a habit. They'd be clumsy to run in.

"Something else, Billy. We both look pretty rough. No shaves. These prison clothes I'm wearing. If we have to run for it we don't have a chance."

"Looks like ol' fat man goin' to have to go to sleep for a while."

"I hate to use force. I'm a completely innocent joker, but if I muss up a cop in a jail break they'll put me away for a year on general principles even after I'm cleared on this other stuff. Same way with you. I hate to do it."

"We'll come back from the cafe before four-thirty, the relief comes on at six. We could use that hour and a half, pardner."

"I'm just guessing at the times."

"What about those drunks in the other cell? They've been sleeping all day. I thought he was going to put them to work. When do they get fed?"

"All we can do, Billy, is try it."

"O.K., pardner."

Billy folded the flash paper into the hinges, showed me how to set them so that the turning hinge would pinch the small caps and set off the flash. Then we went to our bunks and waited. If the fat man came by he wouldn't see us talking together.

The drunks in the other cell finally woke up. They began yelling, so the fat man came and took them off. I guessed that they'd be mopping up the police headquarters in the big building next door. It must have been about four when he came back to our cell."Work, you stand at the rear wall. Don't make any moves." He opened the door and motioned Billy to come out. I was being treated like a real dangerous character. As far as they knew, I was.

When they had disappeared I went to work, setting the flash paper in the hinges. Once, back at the Punchbowl, I had felt like this. My squad had been at one end of a steep, narrow valley. The Reds had come down the slope behind us and we were going to have to fight our way out. It was the same tense feeling now.

The flash papers were ready. When the door opened the hinges would crush the tiny caps. I sat on my bunk and waited. A couple of years went by.

Then I heard footsteps and the fat man waddled up to the cell door. Billy was behind him, carrying a paper bag. It looked like scant rations for me.

The bolt squeaked and the door began to swing open.

There were two pops, two bright flashes of light.

"Hey!" The fat man turned his head and I was on him, pulling him by his shirt in one quick jerk. I swung past him and slammed the door. He was reaching toward his holster as I turned the big key. I started to run.

"It's O.K., pardner. I got it." Billy waved the jailer's gun.

We ran to the room at the end of the hall in the shed between the old jail and the building where the police officers were.

"Want to try that phone?" whispered Billy, pointing to the desk.

"Can't risk it. Goes through the police switchboard. Leave the gun there."

"How about looking for your clothes and stuff?" Billy put the gun on the desk.

"Take too long. We'd better get out of here."

Back in the cell the fat man was yelling. He had a big voice, but the walls of the ancient jail were thick.

We went out the back door. Two empty police cars were

parked there. I looked inside the nearest one. The ignition key was in the lock.

"We might as well go first class," I said, swinging open the door.

Chapter Fourteen

We climbed into the car. I started it and eased it as quietly as I could away from the curb. The clouds were purple-gray above us, and the cool darkness was edging over Monterey.

The first law officer that saw us would blow the whistle. All the car could do for us was to get us away from the jail fast. Then we would have to ditch it.

Back streets—and I didn't know the tangle of dead-end roads in this hundred-year-old part of Monterey.

The telephone on the dashboard muttered something about Franklin and Tyler Streets, then quieted into a buzz again. I headed the car toward the downtown section.

"You fixing to go to the hospital or you going to phone?" asked Billy. He knew the desperate urgency of time now.

"If I could phone Kearny, maybe at the hospital—"

"You don't have even a dime, do you?"

"No." I wheeled the car into a shadowed street.

"Me neither. But I can get maybe four-five bucks quick."

"How?" We were three blocks from the jail now. Time to ditch the car. I pulled it to the curb.

"Got to go downtown. Can you make out with those pants?"

"Have to." I pushed open the door and got out. The street was empty, a tired old street between tired old houses. We walked toward the glow of lights that was Alvarado, main street of Monterey.

"Where's this money?"

"I'll show you. Kind of a trick, too. Let's cross the street to that big hotel and you'll have phone money faster than a preacher can forget about a banker being drunk."

As we went alongside the stuccoed walls of the hotel, Billy reached high above his head to a ledge over a window. He brought his hand down, a half dollar between his fingers.

"See how easy it is?"

"What the hell—" I began, but I was reaching for the money. We might have an hour, we might have a minute before the silent air around us was filled with police radio alarms and the squad cars would begin their search for us. For Wild Kearny it might already be too late. I was half running toward the entrance of the hotel. Billy hurried along beside me.

"When I first hit a new town, if I have any scratch I put a few bucks in silver all over downtown, high up where it can't be seen. It's like a sort of bank. Usually I remember all the places."

The clerk looked up as we entered the lobby. He didn't seem too surprised at my flopping denims or Billy's jeans, shirt, and green bow tie. Lot of sport fishing in Monterey, and even nice people dress oddly there. There was a row of booths near the newsstand. I got change from the girl at the stand and went to a booth.

It was hard to dial the number.

"Monterey Community Hospital, good evening."

"Is Mr. Kearny there? His daughter is a patient."

"One moment, please."

It was one pure hell of a long moment.

Another voice. "Who is calling?"

This was no time for nonsense. "Work. Jim Work."

"Oh." There was a long silence.

The nurse's voice again. "You want to speak to Mr. Kearny?"

Something sounded wrong. "Yes."

"Are you calling him for his daughter?"

"Isn't she there at the hospital?"

Long silence, more whispering, and then, "If you have any information on Miss Kearny, or if you know where she is, you'll have to tell us. It's most important."

"She isn't there?"

"She disappeared more than an hour ago. Where are you calling from?"

"Is her father there?"

"No."

I hung up.

She'd run away. She'd been forced to leave either by violence or by some kind of argument. Her father had taken her away. One of the three—it had to be one of those three explanations.

Which one? And what do I do now?

I pushed open the booth door, stepped out. Billy was showing the rose and egg tricks to the girl behind the newsstand. She was giggling.

"Everything O.K., pardner?

"I don't know."

Billy put his tricks back in his little box.

"Better be moving along, maybe?"

"Let's go," I said. Go where?

I could walk back to the jail, turn myself in. Then the stone walls would box me in again and I would be helpless. Song as I was out, no matter how loud and close the hounds, I wasn't completely helpless.

"You're on your own now, Billy," I told him as we walked into the cool evening darkness outside.

"Did you reach the hospital O.K.?"

"She isn't there. They're looking for her."

"Maybe her old man gimmicked her out.

"I hope he did. But if he didn't—"

We walked toward Alvarado again, not speaking.

Billy stopped about a hundred feet from the corner. "Here's another spot." This time he brought down three quarters that had been hidden behind an awning bracket. "We better do something about getting away, pardner. This town's going to heat up awful fast for us right soon now.

"You take off, Billy."

"Hate to leave you, pardner."

"You want to get out of town. I've got to stick here and find out—"

"O.K., Jim." Billy held out his hand, and as I shook it he gave me his three quarters. "I got lots more around. Just remember Dooley the Fantastic."

He walked away, bowlegged in his tight jeans, a giant elf who would never let the world mean more to him than an audience to be amused. I stood at the corner for a moment watching him. He was more than a hundred feet away when the police car coming toward him pulled sharply to the curb. Two officers were out, guns toward Billy, before the car stopped. Some woman on the sidewalk screamed. Billy stood there, hands high.

I turned back on darker Franklin, not running. I had maybe ten or fifteen seconds to get out of sight. At the corner I turned right and ran past a used-car lot, past the rear entrances of the

Alvarado Street bars.

There was a wooden stairway leading up to old flats above the stores of Alvarado. I went up the stairway.

This was a back porch, two windows and a door opening on it. I tried the door. It was locked. A searchlight swept across the store fronts on the other side of the street. The police car, with Dooley inside, was hunting for me now.

One of the windows was half open. I climbed through it just before the searchlight swept across the porch.

This was a tiny bedroom, empty and dark. I opened the door in the far wall.

"Well, I'll be damned. A burglar!"

Two girls were looking at me. One of them, a full-bodied redhead, was wearing a man's pajama coat, much too large for her, with the sleeves rolled up on her arms. She was holding an opened can of beer.

The other girl wore a half slip and a bra. She had crisp, black hair and a delicate, sculptured face.

They weren't frightened, only annoyed, a little amused maybe. The redhead put down her can of beer and stood there looking at me, her hands on her hips.

"What's the idea, guy?"

"I'm sorry. I'll go." I was surprised at the calmness of both girls.

"Damn right you'll go. But what the hell did you come in here for? You look like a bum. What are you, prowling for food or money or something?" The redhead walked up to me, her hands still on her hips. I thought she might be drunk, but she wasn't. Just annoyed and curious, more curious than annoyed.

"Give the guy a break," said the slim, dark-haired girl. "He doesn't look tough, just kinda scared."

"Walking in on us like he owned the joint. I ought to call the cops," said the redhead. She was in her middle twenties, with everything a little big in her face, big eyes, big nose, big mouth, but handsome.

"I made a mistake." I started to close the door and the redhead grabbed it.

"Just a minute, fella. You come in here. We won't bite you."

The dark bedroom behind me brightened for an instant.

They were still hunting me, the squad car's searchlight

fingering across the shadowed porches.

I shrugged. "The cops are looking for me." It was only a question of seconds anyway.

"Yeah? Why?" The redhead motioned me into the cluttered living room.

"My name's Work. They think I killed a girl."

The two girls looked at each other. "In Carmel, last night?"

"That's right."

The dark-haired girl picked up an iron from the table behind her.

"Tell us about it," said the redhead. Her face was inches from mine, her big eyes wide.

"Didn't do it. Long story."

"Are the cops hot after you now?"

I motioned toward the street back of me. "Out there."

The dark-haired girl put the iron back on the table. "Shall I call 'em, Dee?"

"What do you think, kid?" asked the redhead.

"Give the guy a break. Let him move on out of here and we forget we saw him."

"Want a can of beer, fella?" asked Dee.

"Sure." These were sort of Chicago-style girls, the kind you find behind the Twenty-six game in the taverns. I could understand why they hadn't been frightened or excited when a stranger walked in on them. They were completely confident of their ability to handle almost any situation.

"You girls in show business?"

Dee nodded. She was opening another can of beer, taking it from a carton of six on the table. "I sing. Not too good, but plenty loud. Marcy's a cocktail waitress. Here's your beer fella."

"Thanks." I drank it from the can and it tasted fine.

Dee walked past me into the bedroom. Marcy got out of the chair and came over to me.

"What's with the elephant-sized clothes?"

"Jail clothes," I answered. "I broke out a few minutes ago."

"We don't want to be rude or anything," said Marcy, "but after you finish the beer maybe you'd better travel. The law might take it wrong if they found you here."

Bang-bang-bang. Somebody was knocking on a door in the front of the tiny apartment, at the end of a short hall.

"Hell," said Marcy. "Duck, kid. I'll answer it."

I went into the bedroom. Dee was pulling on some clothes.

"Now what?" she said. "Will you kindly stop roaming around our apartment?"

"Somebody at the door. Marcy answered it."

"Probably the cops. What's she going to tell them? That you're here?"

"I don't know."

"I guess not. She's too damn kindhearted for her own good. This place'd be crawling with stray dogs, cats, and wounded birds if I let her."

"Figure me as one of the stray dogs. I'm no wounded bird."

"Are you going to stand there and watch me get dressed? I'm a singer, not a stripper, laddie-boy."

I went back into the living room. Marcy was closing the front door. She put a finger to her lips.

"Who was it, hon?" called Dee.

"Cops. Warning us there was a desperate killer maybe in this block."

"This fella? Maybe it's those crazy pants, but he doesn't look desperate to me."

"Finish your beer and take your time, now. Better give the law a chance to go somewhere else," said Marcy.

"Where you from, guy?" asked Dee. She was looking at her face in the mirror.

"Chicago."

"Good town. Kind of dirty, but the people are fun. Used to sing at a tavern out on West Seventy-Ninth." She was exploring her mouth with a finger. "Gah cawy," she mumbled. Out came the finger and she smiled. "I said I've got a cavity. Better I should see a dentist."

"You've been saying that for six months." Marcy laughed. "Hey, I'd better start dressing now. I go to work at six. Another night of shoulder-grabbers and fanny-patters. Ah, me.

I finished my can of beer. "You girls got something I could use for a belt?"

"Hell," said Marcy, "I'll give you a whole outfit, and I think it'll fit you. Some of my damn ex-husband's stuff. Glad to get rid of it."

"Where's he at?"

"Jail. Where else?"

"Hell of a charming guy," said Dee. "Marcy was kind of crazy about him, in a kind of crazy way, I suppose. But he was a real lush. Never could understand a man who liked whisky better than women.

"I can," Marcy called from a closet. "Some whisky and some women. She came back with a coat and trousers. "Here, try these on. I'll get the shirt and the rest of the junk. You got the stuff on underneath that frantic outfit?"

"Suppose you give us the real scoop on what happened last night," Dee said.

"It was a man named Buddy Brown."

"The radio didn't mention Buddy Brown," said Dee. "Do you mean a tall, wide-shouldered, skinny guy with real black eyes?"

"That's the one. You know him?"

"Damn right I know him."

"Here?"

"L.A. He a friend of yours?

"We each hate the way the other guy breathes."

"That's nice," said Dee, smashing out a cigarette. "He's a real fine person—to hate."

I began to change clothes.

"Go on. Tell us the story," Marcy said. "I'll whip us up a few corned-beef sandwiches and some more beer."

"It started yesterday. I was in Carmel...."

But as I talked, the question was pounding within me: Where is Wild?

Chapter Fifteen

The sandwiches were good and I needed mine. They listened to the story carefully, asking questions now and then.

"You really all gone for this girl?"

I buttoned Marcy's ex-husband's shirt. It fitted well, a wine-red tab-collar job.

"I'm gone for her."

Dee was pulling on her stockings. The three of us were finishing dressing, eating our sandwiches, drinking beer as I talked. We could have been three people in a carnie, not bothered, not bothering.

"Why?"

"She was exciting from the second I saw her. She's never stopped being exciting, and she never will for me. That good enough?"

"I get guys excited, but it never seems to last," Dee said.

"You don't mind about this Brown?" Marcy asked.

"Of course I mind," I answered. "Plenty. But that's got nothing to do with us. I love the girl."

"So now what are you going to do?"

"Find her. Get the facts so the law will leave us alone."

"Sounds all right if you don't have much else to do tonight."

I finished tying the knit-silver bow Marcy had picked for me. It wasn't bad. I looked a little too sharp, but it was better than the tent-sized denims.

"Do you think she's got much interest in you?" Marcy asked.

"If a man starts worrying about that—" I began.

Marcy shook her head. "Don't bother, kid. You're right."

"You're a dreamer," Dee said, putting down her can of beer. "I've heard about this Broadway Red Kearny. He's loaded. He'll hide her out in some fancy resort hotel until his lawyers and private dicks handle everything. Then off to Paris for his daughter. There'll be no more loving for you, poor dreamer. What you've got, kid, is memories. Memories and a mess of cops on your tail."

I didn't say anything.

"This Brown," she continued, "that's different. It couldn't happen to a sweeter person, what's going to happen to him. Kearny'll have his boys kill him like a farmer kills a rat.

"I'll tell you about Brown. I used to sing in a joint way west on Santa Monica down in L.A. Place got a big play from a bunch of kids who thought they were real cool hipsters. Brown hung around there and picked them off like grapes—the girls. Sometimes one of these kids would have a boy friend or something who'd get sore when he found that Buddy had turned the girl into a dopey-eyed hustler. Brown loved that. I'll give him credit, he's plenty tough. He'd work the guy over like a butcher. One of the girls told me the only time she'd ever seen Buddy look content was when he was marking a boy up for life. She'd done plenty herself to try to make him look that way, but it never worked. A girl can't do it for him."

"You'd better shave," said Marcy. "There's a razor and things in the bathroom."

I went in. I found the razor and pushed the drying stockings out of my way so I could see the mirror.

"I've known a lot of bad ones," Dee called toward me, "but Brown is the pure quill when it comes to being bad."

There was a man's face in the mirror. A tired face. Jim Work, who hadn't had a worry in the world thirty-six hours ago. But he hadn't had Wild Kearny then, either.

I started to shave. The razor pulled like an old rake in high weeds.

"Personally, I don't think a girl who's fooled around with Buddy is ever much good afterward," said Dee. I could hear Marcy trying to shush her.

"He seems like a nice guy," Dee said to Marcy. "and he's in a big enough jam right now without having to eat his heart out over one of that rat's tomatoes. I've seen too many of them."

I finished shaving and went back into the other room. Marcy had finished dressing and she wore a lacy black evening gown. Dee had on something in green, off the shoulders; she was good-looking in an easygoing, strong-bodied way.

"You got a phone?" I asked.

"Sure. Want it private?" Marcy asked. There was something in her eyes as she looked at me that said she'd wait around until

I was out of my jam and maybe in the market again. Then she'd be there.

"I'm going to call the cops," I said.

"Not from here, you aren't, honey," said Dee. "I think you're in a bum deal and we're glad to help you. It's real interesting. But you don't get us in no wringer with the law. If you want to call the cops, do it from the drugstore—and when you leave here, please remember to forget that you ever saw us. O.K.?"

""Wish my goddamn husband could see you in that suit," said Marcy, putting her hands on my lapels. "He always looked like he needed some more padding on the shoulders."

"What you want to call the law for, friend?" asked Dee.

"I figured a gimmick. I'm going to say I'm calling from the city room of one of the San Francisco papers."

"And you want the latest scoop on the Brooks killing. That's kind of clever."

"If they know where your girl is, for example," said Marcy.

"I want to know who this witness is. Then I can do me some action."

"Call away. Better let me pretend I'm the long-distance operator."

The phone was on a table in the corner. Dee looked up the number and dialed it.

"This is San Francisco," she said when she had an answer, and her voice was changed now, it had the mechanical quality of a telephone operator. "I have a call for the chief of police at Carmel." She waited for a few seconds, listened, and then said, "Here is your party. Go ahead, please." She handed the phone to me.

"Hello." It was Clyde.

"San Francisco Examiner," I said, speaking crisply.

"Yes?"

"What's the news on that Brooks affair?"

"There's a lot of news," Clyde answered. "The man we think is the killer escaped from the Monterey police an hour or so ago. You've got his name?"

"James Work. That the man?"

"Right. He and a cellmate, a kid who stole a car, broke out. They captured the kid—William Dooley, a transient—about half an hour ago in downtown Monterey. Work is still on the loose."

"You're sure he killed the Brooks girl?"

"Looks that way. You know he accused a fellow named Brown?"

"We got all that this morning.

"Brown's got a solid alibi. He's clean."

"Who is his alibi?" This was the big question.

"Couple of people. What makes it solid is Mrs. Worton Henderville." Clyde spoke as if I'd know the name.

"I see. Anything else?"

"Lots. This thing is getting very odd. The other girl involved, Wild Kearny, disappeared from a local hospital this afternoon. Apparently just walked away. You'd think somebody would see her—tall, beautiful girl with hardly any clothes on, just a hospital nightgown. But she walked away."

"Do you think her father is involved in that?"

"No. That's another odd thing. You know who he is—a New York gambler and union boss. Not a hoodlum, but with lots of hoodlum connections. Very rich. This afternoon, just about the time his daughter was getting ready to do her vanishing act, we got a telegram from New York to take this man Kearny into custody."

"Kearny?"

"Yes. We arrested him this afternoon and took him to Salinas for the U.S. District Marshal. He'll be on his way back to New York tomorrow to face income-tax-evasion charges."

"With his daughter missing and mixed up in a murder?"

"It's tough, but we had to do it. When Uncle Sam says to arrest 'em, we just go out and bring 'em in. It took three deputies to put the cuffs on Kearny, too. He was like a crazy man."

"Yeah, I can understand." I said.

"But this case is still breaking. You've got the picture? A girl from a rich Eastern society family murdered. The killer escaped from jail. The girl we suspect was involved in the killing escaped from the hospital. Her father arrested for income-tax evasion. Now we find out that this fellow Work is involved in the biggest dope ring on the West Coast."

"What?"

"That's right. This ex-soldier just back from Korea smuggled in a big load of Japanese heroin. At least five thousand dollars' worth at wholesale prices—maybe would sell to addicts for fifty thousand or more. We've got a man hunt started for that fellow that will sew up the Monterey Peninsula tighter than a rat trap. Shoot to kill, if necessary."

"Give me the story on this dope angle. That's brand-new."

"Sorry. You can say that we know he's involved and that's all. We've got the evidence and we're holding back until we can get the rest of the gang."

"Can't you give me anything more?"

"Sorry. Try the folks at the Federal Narcotics Office in San Francisco tomorrow. They're hot on it and we're playing ball with them."

"Thanks," I said, and hung up. Five thousand dollars' worth of narcotics! Me—a dope smuggler!

"What's the matter, dreamer? You don't look happy."

I turned to Dee and Marcy. "The law's got me pegged for being a dope smuggler as well as a murderer," I said.

Dee's big eyes narrowed to slits. "You mixed up with that stuff?"

"No. Flat no. Never."

"Why do the Dick Tracys think you are?"

"They won't say. But they sounded awful sure." I sat down.

"Did you find out who the witness is?"

"Never heard of her. A Mrs. Worton Henderville."

Dee's eyes widened. "Marcy, we've been taken. This guy is guilty as hell."

"Hey!" I said. I could see that she wasn't joking.

"Look, guy," said Dee. "I know Mrs. Henderville. She comes into the Gilded Cage with her friends and sometimes she asks me to do special numbers for her. She's nearly sixty. She's very wealthy—has a big house in Pebble Beach. She's a nice, smart, decent old lady who never told a lie in her life. If she says you're lying, then you're lying."

"Take it easy," Marcy said. "I still believe the guy."

Dee lit a cigarette, blew out smoke. "Mrs. Henderville is the alibi for Buddy Brown—is that right?"

"That's what the cops say. She'll testify that he was someplace where she was around three o'clock this morning. That's when I found Brown standing over Pen Brooks in the bedroom."

Dee stubbed out the cigarette. "It doesn't figure. Mrs. Henderville isn't the kind to be mixed up with Buddy Brown, not for one second. She's too nice."

"Could she be on a dope kick?" asked Marcy.

Dee shook her head. "When she comes to the Gilded Cage he's always with a party of rich old folks like herself. One of them is her family doctor. He'd know if there was anything wrong with her. There isn't, I guarantee that."

"But she's lying." I said.

"She doesn't lie."

"Then she's been fooled."

"That would be one hard old lady to fool."

"What's the news on your girl, Wild?" asked Marcy.

I stood up. "No news. She walked out this afternoon in her nightgown. Nobody's seen her since. And her father's in jail in Salinas on federal income-tax charges. He can't get bail here and they'll take him to New York tomorrow."

"You sure don't go around with a very nice crowd, do you?" said Marcy. "Two of you on the lam, one in the cooler. You turn out to be the biggest hoodlum since Mickey Cohen, and the chief witness that you're a liar is the nicest old lady west of the Statue of Liberty, according to Dee, who doesn't fool easy." She opened three more cans of bees. "If you didn't look so sweet in my damn ex-husband's clothes, I'd be in favor of yelling for the cops myself."

Dee drank her beer, wiped her lips. "O.K., buster. You're on your own. If it wasn't that Buddy Brown's mixed up in this, I'd be blowing the whistle right now to have this place belly-deep in cops. But even Mrs. Henderville will never convince this girl that Buddy isn't the dirtiest rat in California. So take off, buster."

I walked toward the hallway.

"Got any idea what you're going to do?" asked Marcy, following me.

"I know what I've got to do." I took her hand. "You girls have been great. If you hadn't gone along—"

"Skip it," Marcy said. "When you aren't hot, look me up sometime. I'd like to see that technique of yours in action."

I walked out the front door and down the stairs to the street. At about the same place on the Alvarado sidewalk where Billy had been picked up a police cruiser passed me. The officer on the right side looked at me and looked away.

In my pocket was about a dollar in coins that Dooley had given me. I knew where I was going and what I was going to do.

Chapter Sixteen

Five thousand dollars' worth of Japanese heroin. That's what Clyde had said. Last night, when he was drunk and panic-yellow, Brown had talked about five thousand dollars. It was only a mixed-up thought as I went along.

I turned off Alvarado and walked to the Bay Rapid bus station. Twenty-five cents would get me into Carmel. It was a thousand to one that Wild Kearny was in Carmel, and I had to find her fast.

Fifteen minutes after I got there the big white Carmel bus rolled into the station, and I got aboard. I watched the neon signs of the stores flashing red, yellow, and green as the bus moved toward Carmel.

In no time at all, it seemed, the bus was on Ocean Avenue in Carmel. I got off and crossed the street to Whitney's, a red-and-white-fronted restaurant and bar. The bar was in front, small and U-shaped, with tables around the walls. Maybe fifteen people were in the place.

"Beer," I said to the barman.

As the barman poured the beer I said, "I'm looking for a fellow named Buddy Brown. You know him?"

The barman looked at me with open curiosity. "Yeah, sure. He comes in here sometimes."

"Know where I can find him?"

The place was completely silent.

"You a friend of his?"

"No."

"Newspaperman?"

"That's right."

"Yeah. You might be wasting your time; the story around town is that he had nothing to do with that murder. He was somewhere else."

Carmel is a little town where people in the half-dozen or so bars spend much of their long drinking days talking about each other. The stabbing of Pen Brooks would be a big, big thing to the talkers in the bars. In one way and another they'd know most of the story by the time their second Martini was down to the olive.

"He was?"

"Yeah. Rich old doll and her son say he was with them last night until about four this morning. She's the kind of old doll everybody believes. You know the girl and the guy both escaped?"

"Yes. We got a flash on it."

"Damnedest thing you ever heard. She was in the hospital with a cop outside the door—I'll be right with you, sir—and when the nurse came back the girl was gone. Took off in her nightie."

"Find her yet?"

The barman mixed a Martini. "Nope. She's wandering around like that, barefooted, practically nothing on. You'd sure think somebody would spot her."

On a stool around the corner of the bar a big man chuckled. "That's one beautiful girl, but she never did seem to like clothes too much. During that warm spell a little time back she used to come down Ocean in shorts. Real short shorts."

"Had real long legs, too. Gorgeous legs. Don't blame her for wearing shorts. Ought to be a law requiring a girl with legs like that to wear shorts," said a sandy-haired man in a loud sports jacket.

"You're the boy to notice 'em, Jackson," said the barman. Everybody laughed except me.

"Where can I find this Buddy Brown?"

"You rented him the place," the barman said to the sandy-haired man.

"Yeah. About a block from here, down Carada. Right next to the corner where the big ravine cuts through. Redwood, green shingles."

"Thanks." I finished my beer. There was no way of even starting to look for Wild, but if Brown was home...

It was dark off the main street on Carada. I was worried about a police stake-out at Brown's house. They might figure me to come here, even figure Wild to go to Brown. Cautiously I walked along Carada, passed the house on the corner. There was a light behind drapery-covered windows. No cars nearby.

I walked through the tangle of flowers around the side of

the small house.

Wooden shutters covered a side window. I stumbled over a heap of branches and climbed a low stucco wall. Now I was at the rear of the house. A steep ravine cut off the ground here, and I could see the lights of houses at the bottom, twenty feet or more below me.

The window at the back of the cottage was a large single pane of glass, without curtains or draperies. I could see into the long main room of Buddy Brown's home. There was light from a lamp near the door, and I saw bottles on a coffee table near a big couch, a couple of chairs, another couch that was probably a bed in the corner. One corner of the room near my window was cut off by a wall, and I guessed that the bathroom and whatever kitchen he had were behind this wall.

The big room was empty. I waited outside in the darkness, the brush-tangled ravine behind me.

This was my only point of contact. I could try the mysterious and respectable Mrs. Henderville, but she lived in Pebble Beach, behind the guarded gates of Del Monte Properties, impossible to get to without a car.

I could try to search the hundred back streets of night-shrouded Carmel for a barefoot girl in a hospital nightgown, but the police were doing that.

This was the only point of contact I had.

Maybe it was an hour. It was a long, measureless time in the cool, purple dark. Then some animal was coming through the winter-dried brush of the ravine, slowly. I turned to look for it and I saw her, a slim ghost.

Wild Kearny was climbing the side of the ravine, ghost-pale in the faint light from the houses.

She couldn't see me against the darkness of the wall, but now she was close, coming over the tall grass at the edge of the black incline.

I could hear a car stopping in front of Brown's cottage. "Better give it another check all around," a man's voice called. A flashlight beam brightened a circle of bushes behind the corner house.

"I still don't think that girl could make it over here in her bare feet. It's a helluva cold night!" answered the man with the light.

Carmel police hunting for Wild Kearny at Buddy Brown's—and they were right. Somehow she had come through the wooded hills of the night-black village toward the house of the man I knew would kill her.

She saw the light, heard the voices. The slim ghost vanished against the edge of the ravine.

The beam of light traversed the bushes beyond the stucco wall and then it flickered out.

"Damn!"

"What's the matter?" the man in front yelled back.

"Light's gone sour. I think it's the bulb."

"I've got a spare in the kit."

I could hear the officer tramping through the pile of branches next to the house. Bending low, I half ran, half crawled to the place where Wild was flattened against the ground in the high, dry grass.

"It's Jim, Wild," I whispered.

Her face was a faint silver oval. I straightened myself on the ground next to her, one hand on her back. "It's Jim," I whispered again.

The muscles of her shoulder were quivering. We were side by side in the tall, crisp slivers of grass; by lifting my head I could see the glow of the window in the rear wall of the cottage. The flashlight beam came again, wavering as the policeman stumbled along the side of the cottage, climbed the wall.

"Don't talk, don't move," I whispered close to Wild's ear.

The flashlight swept across the grass at the top of the ravine, searched out the wall, the bushes. We could see him, like a shadow, across the window glow as he peered in. He called something back to the man in front, and then went around the side.

In the still, cool blackness we could hear the police car start and pull away.

"Wild, are you all right?" I tried to see her face.

"I'm terribly hungry," she said as she pulled herself up.

I stood and took her by the shoulders. "Why did you run away from the hospital? Had the police talked to you?"

"There was a doctor. He wouldn't let me talk to anybody. They said my father was outside, and then when I asked for him they told me he was gone. I had to get away."

"You've been out—like this—for hours?"

"There were French doors on my room. I just walked out and then I knew I would have to hide. There was a garage behind a house and I hid there until it was dark. When it was dark I started to walk here, hiding in the bushes and behind trees if there were cars on the roads. Now I'm hungry."

"Why here, Wild? You know he killed Pen." I was still holding her by the shoulders as we stood in the dry grass above the houses in the ravine. I could see her face in the glow from the window.

"Nobody would tell me anything. How Pen was. You say she's dead. I didn't know. This was the only place I could go. I had to find out about Pen. About my father. About Buddy. I couldn't go to the Zoo, never again. But there would be a phone here, and I could find out. They wouldn't tell me at the hospital. They wouldn't tell me anything."

"Pen died today. Your father is in trouble—income taxes. Buddy is free and on the town."

"Buddy? With Pen dead? Did they think it was an accident?"

"They think either you or I stabbed her." Her body was still trembling. I could feel the thin, harsh hospital cotton nightgown on her shoulders.

"I broke out of jail, Wild. I came here to get Brown before he could kill you."

"Buddy—kill me? Why?"

"He was gone before the doctor or the police arrived. He's got a witness to say he was never near the Zoo that night. He's afraid the police might believe you, and most of all he's afraid of your father."

"My father—where is he?"

"I told you. In trouble. Held by the federal marshal in Salinas on tax charges."

"He knew that was coming. That was one reason he came here—to make sure I'd be all right if there was trouble. He'll get out. He always does." She sounded very tired.

"But Wild, you're sick. You've got to get warm, get some food, have medical care."

"I can take care of myself. I'm going into Buddy's house." She pulled herself away from me. "One thing I remember, Jim.

I remember you."

"You said you hated me." We were standing a little apart, facing each other.

"I was in that hospital bed looking at the ceiling for a long time today. There were things to think about. Buddy. Pen. You. I don't hate you, Jim. It was all pretty dirty. I wish you had met me three weeks ago. I wish I'd never met Buddy. I wish a lot of things."

I went to her and took her in my arms.

"Most of all, Jim, I wished it hadn't been a lie to my father yesterday. If it had only been true, things wouldn't be dirty, would they."

"We'll make out," I said, and I kissed her.

Her slim, strong body in the torn rough nightgown wasn't trembling now.

"I'm going to break into Brown's house. It's the only thing we can do. I'll call somebody who can get us help. Pete Barrow or somebody who knows you. Once they understand what happened last night, we'll be fine."

We climbed the top of the ravine and I went to the big window. It was hinged from the top so that it could be swung up and open. I hit it with the heel of my hand until I broke the catch and then I pried it open. I lifted Wild in my arms. She pushed up the window as I held her and slid in, dropping to the floor. I climbed through after her.

Now we were together in the light. Wild's nightgown was badly torn, very dirty. She was rubbing the soles of her bare feet, and they were dirty, too.

"You walked barefoot?"

"It wasn't bad. In the summer I usually do. Tough feet." She managed to smile. "There's only one thing that will do me any good now—a shower."

I took her in my arms again. What I had known by instinct yesterday was certain now. This was the only girl that would ever be important to me. For better or for worse.

I let her go and for a moment she looked away from me, looked at Buddy's room. She shivered and her head turned.

"It's all right, Wild," I said.

She looked up at me. "All right, Jim."

She put out her hand, we each felt the pressure of the other for a moment, and then she went into the bathroom.

I heard the splash of the shower and I stood alone. We'd fight our way out of this. It wasn't a bad jam once it started straightening out.

The front door clicked, swung open, and Buddy Brown was there. We stared at each other.

I moved toward him and he dropped his right hand to his pocket. He came forward with a thin, long knife ready for me.

"Sucker," he said in a bitter voice. "This was the last place you should have come."

He'd kicked the door shut and we faced each other. The splash of the shower was the only sound.

"I'm going to kill you, sucker." He heard the sound of the water now and I could see his body tighten. I moved toward him; we were maybe ten feet apart now. The knife was bright for a moment as it caught the light, a four-inch, slender blade pointed forward and upward.

"She's here," he said. "It has to be her." The black eyes searched out mine. "I'll kill you and then I can handle her, sucker. I'll hurt her and she'll love it. I know her, and I know she loves it."

We were six feet apart, both of us moving very slowly, both of us on the balls of our feet. Both of my hands, fingers open, were chest high, a little forward. I was trying to get his eyes again, but they would flicker up for a moment, look down.

"I know her, sucker. She's crazy about me when I kick her around. Crazy for it."

This was the time now. We were close enough, four feet apart. The knife was lowering a little, pointing flat and straight toward my belly now.

"Sucker!" he hissed, and struck.

I went to the left, chopping down with my right hand toward his wrist. The knife missed and I swung in with my left hand, trying to find his wrist with my right. The knife was coming forward and I fell back, stumbled, went over.

I kicked him away. He was standing, knife ready, smiling. I was on my back, looking up at him.

He was in no hurry and I had to wait for his move.

He was a knife fighter; he would know how to handle himself against an unarmed man flat on his back. I could kick, grab, roll, try to throw myself up—but that blade would find my belly, my throat.

He picked up a silver cigarette case from the low table with his left hand and threw it at my face. I rolled and the box hit my shoulder heavy and hard. He was on me. I kicked and missed as he came down, knife arm close to his body, left hand reaching for my face.

The knife caught me at the top of the throat, just the bite of the point as my head went back, my hands grabbing his wrist. He leaned on me, putting his weight on his stiff right arm, and the point bit hot and wet.

My hands and wrists fought his arm, fought his muscles, fought his weight, a tight, close struggle of breath-deep fractions of an inch.

And then black hot eyes looked away and over his shoulders I could see Wild like a glistening golden statue above him, a statue of a Valkyrie fighter.

I twisted his hand back against his wrist as his weight lifted for a moment, brought my left fist solid against the bridge of his nose. The knife slithered away and I rolled with him, locking my right arm around his head, twisting myself to get above him.His whole body jerked once, and I let him fall away from me, his eyes wide, white now. I pushed him and his head fell against his shoulder.

We still looked each other in the eyes as he died there, his neck broken.

Chapter Seventeen

My hand was against the cut in my throat. She was standing back, hands at her sides, her golden body wet, her head down.

He was dead. The few nervous, hot-blooded years, the twisted hungers, the caged-animal hate—all over.

"How badly did he hurt you?" she said, looking up, her hands out to me.

It took a moment to talk. "A cut. Nothing. He's dead."

We both looked at the man. He had meant a kind of love to her, a terrible thing of passion-whipped senses. A dozen nights of laughter and white-hot nerves, hot black eyes and a mocking mouth. But love.

He had meant hate to me from the moment we met.

I shook my head the way a fighter does after a bad round.

Her arms were around me, sensitive fingers touching the bleeding hole in my throat. "It wasn't really killing," she said.

"I would have killed him with my hands, with a knife, with a gun, with a whip."

For a long time we were silent, but we were close.

I dropped my arms from her and pushed her back.

"You'll have to get away from here, Wild. I'm going to call them before they come here again, looking for you. You'll have to be gone—and you never were here, not tonight."

"How bad is this, Jim?"

"Real bad, Wild. I'll get a lawyer and maybe somebody will believe me—I don't know. They were pretty sure that one of us, you or I, stabbed Pen. With Brown dead, what can I say now? I killed him."

"If you hadn't, maybe I would have done it," Wild said, and she pointed to the floor. "When I heard the noise over the splashing, I looked out and saw you on the floor, and he had the knife over you. I brought that from the shelf."

It was a straight-edged razor, bright and deadly, on the floor.

"You would have killed—him? To save me?" She pointed

again to the razor and then she began to sob, covering her face with her hands, dry, soundless sobs that shook her body.

I waited for her to be done. When she was ready for my arms she put down her hands. I held her tightly, as if I could bring us together above flesh or life, and she said, "That's the way it is, Jim.

"That's the way it is, Wild."

A tiredness of cold, liquid lead was rising in me, as if I were a grotesque, man-shaped empty bottle slowly being filled with it. I fought it off. Wild and I would have to work for our lives now. We were looking into short weeks and endless years, the two of us. Short weeks to the tiled room at San Quentin with the curious, terrible faces looking through the thick glass window as I waited on my chair. Endless years in stiff, shapeless prison clothes for lovely Wild Kearny.

"Get some clothes on," I said to Wild, and I spoke sharply; there could be no tenderness of love for us until there was nothing, no other hope, left for us.

"I—have some here, Jim."

"Get them on, and hurry." There was no time for jealousy of a dead man.

While she dressed I went into the little bathroom, turned off the shower, closed the razor, and put it back on the shelf. I put a Band-Aid on my throat.

She would leave, I would wait a little while and then call my friend Clyde. I wondered if I would see Billy Dooley again. Probably not, unless it was in a jailhouse corridor.

Wild was dressed now in a deep-toned print dress, a pattern from the Islands, and very pretty.

"You look wonderful, Wild." It was a good thing to say. She needed words like that.

"Jim, you say my father's in Salinas?"

"I guess in the county jail, being held for the federal marshal. They'll take him to New York tomorrow."

"If I call him from here they might trace the call."

"It doesn't matter. I'm going to call them anyway."

"Couldn't we escape, Jim? Get away from here? Once my father's in New York, he'll get out on bail. He'll hire the best lawyers, use influence. It would be better if you could hide someplace until they know the truth."

"The truth that I killed him?"

"That was self-defense. He had a knife, he would have killed you. There are fingerprints, the wound on your throat."

"They'll say I faked them, cut myself. It would be easy to do."

"Jim, you said Buddy had a witness. Who is it?"

"Some rich old lady in Pebble Beach who's got a better reputation than an archbishop. Her name's Henderville. Mrs. Worton Henderville."

Astonishment opened Wild's mouth, widened her eyes.

"Mrs. Henderville?"

"That's right. Know her?"

"Pete Barrow is her son by her first marriage. She says Buddy was with her?"

"I pretended I was a newspaper reporter and called the Carmel police. That's what they told me."

"But Pete and Buddy weren't even friends, not even before Buddy—" She didn't finish the sentence.

"The chief said there were two witnesses. They would be Pete and his mother."

"Jim, we'll have to see them. Tonight. It's a chance."

"They'd just call the cops and that would be it. You get out of here, Wild."

She didn't answer. She went to the front window, pulled the drapes aside enough to look out, and shielded her eyes against the light from the lamp. Then she walked back to where Brown was crumpled and I saw her lift her chin high, close her eyes, clench her hands, breathe deeply once. She let the air out in a soft sigh and bent over Buddy. Her hand went into his trouser pocket and came out with a jingle of keys.

"The MG is in front. Let's go, Jim."

It would be better than calling, waiting for them.

We turned out the light and left the cottage.

"I'll drive," Wild said. "I know the way."

She pulled away from the curb and almost up to Ocean before she turned on the headlights. "While we're driving, tell me what happened after I fainted last night."

She was hearing about Billy Dooley by the time we climbed the hill. It was exactly nine o'clock then and she turned on the car radio for the news.

"He must be a swell kid," she said. "We've got to help him as soon as we can."

"—and the top local news story is the desperate escape of a murder suspect and a young car thief from the Monterey jail late this afternoon," said the pleasant, mildly enthusiastic voice of the newscaster. "James Work, a recently returned Korea veteran, was held on suspicion of the murder of Penelope Brooks, young artist, in Carmel last night.

"Work, who is believed to have masterminded the smuggling of fifty thousand dollars' worth of heroin from Japan, is still being hunted by Monterey Peninsula authorities. The car thief, William Dooley, was found walking on Alvarado Street in Monterey shortly after the jail break. When questioned about Work's movements after the escape, Dooley told police, Tm a magician. I made him disappear.'

"The Japanese heroin was brought over on the troopship General Hanford by another soldier. Work, who also returned from the Far East on the Hanford, is believed to have picked it up after docking. The heroin was discovered hidden in his car during a police search following the stabbing of Miss Brooks.

"Other news—" I clicked it off.

"Buddy," said Wild. "He had a package in the Zoo he asked Pen and me to keep for him. He must have put it in your car when he walked out last night."

"He didn't have much time."

"It was next to the door in a cabinet."

"He figured the police would search the house anyway, and I guess he thought my car would be safe. It was only worth five thousand wholesale, but that must have been the big score he was talking about."

"Now all we have to do, after we get Pete and his mother to tell the truth, is to tell the police that this was Buddy's package," said Wild, swinging the car into the stone-towered gate of the Del Monte Properties.

"They won't believe you," I said.

Wild stopped the car for the guard and the last two of Dooley's quarters went to him. We didn't dare have him call the Henderville home and ask them if they were expecting guests. Otherwise it costs a half dollar per car to enter the private barony that includes Pebble Beach and the Del Monte Forest.

Wild put the car in gear.

"They won't believe you and these people won't change their story." I felt low. What I had done tonight was with me now and there was no escape from it. Self-defense? Sure, but I felt sick and dirty inside. The clouds had rolled away from the moon and the night was bright with silver now, too beautiful, too unreal.

I knew what reality was.

Around us, almost hidden by the trees, rising up on the hills above the moon-streaked Pacific, were houses warm with lights. Pleasant, secure, comfortable houses, the kind I'd thought about for myself someday.

Wild swung the little car into a short driveway curving before a long, low house built mostly of glass, surrounded by Shasta daisy bushes that seemed to be explosions of white in the moonlight.

Pete's Jaguar was parked behind a Chrysler Imperial, both of them shining with streaks of moon fire.

"We'll play it straight and hard," I said. "They're lying. We know it. Their lies could kill us both—so it's straight and hard."

"We're together, Jim."

Up the broad, low fieldstone steps to the long panels of glass. Wild knew the house. She went to the left, pulled a panel that rolled quietly aside. We went into an enormous room done in gray and green with a round fireplace, hooded in copper, in the center.

Pete Barrow was in a low chair made of shaped wood. He was looking through the glass wall on the other side of the room at the silver, shimmering Pacific. He had a bottle and a half-filled brandy glass on the table beside the chair.

"Hello, Pete," Wild said.

He sat completely still for a long moment and then he stood up and faced us.

"Hello, Wild. It's good to see you," he said. Brush-cut hair, the kind of modern handsome man's face that isn't pretty or soft—rugged lines and tanned, big, tall, muscular body, white teeth, and an automatic smile. The smile was on now, and his eyes moved from Wild to me.

"Did you get out of your troubles, Work?" The laws of his breed made him look at my clothes, the sharpie time-payment clothes of Marcy's ex-husband, and I knew that Pete Barrow would not have worn such clothes even to escape from a pack of bloodhounds.

"Is your mother at home?"

"I don't believe you know my mother." The smile hadn't changed, the voice was pleasant; the remote coldness seemed to seep out of him invisibly.

I took a handful of his soft cashmere sweater, pulled him toward me, and slapped him hard across the face. He pumped three or four short rights and lefts at my body and I swung him into a wrist lock.

A Japanese houseboy peered around a door at the end of the gray-green room, squeaked, and came pattering to his master's aid.

"Hideo!" said Wild sharply. "You get Mrs. Henderville, hayaka!"

Hideo stopped in mid-patter, looked thoughtful and worried, then pattered out of the room. Pete was wiggling. I dropped the wrist lock and put the works into a right that went an inch into the muscle over his heart. He said, "Oof!" and sat down on the floor.

I'd killed a man with my bare hands within the last half hour and the feel of it was in my blood.

"Hello, Mrs. Henderville," said Wild. I turned to look at the woman who stood for a second in the doorway. Dee might call her a nice old lady, but it was a bad description. She was the kind of mother you'd expect to see with her tanned son in the society-page pictures of the horse show or the Pebble Beach sports-car races. Slim, silver-gray hair, a face much like Pete's, tanned, with lines of strength and experience. She was wearing a dark blue suit of something soft and tailored, a pearl-colored sweater of Angora, a necklace of Mexican silver.

She looked at her son, sitting on the floor, and I felt that even when he was a little boy and was hurt she would do as the books said and not rush to him with alarm or sticky sympathy.

"What's the trouble, Pete?" she asked him, still at the end of the room.

"This is the fellow the police want, Sue," he said. He got up, one hand on his stomach.

Sue Barrow Henderville looked at me briefly, to see what I looked like, and then spoke to Wild.

"I believe you're ill, Wild. Do you want to go upstairs and rest?"

"Did you tell the police that Buddy Brown was here last night until four a.m.?"

"Certainly. Why are you interested?"

"Why are you lying?" I asked her.

She didn't bother to look at me, or indicate in any way that she had heard me. I knew that this would be true always. To Mrs. Worton Henderville, Jim Work did not exist.

"You don't talk to my mother like that, fellow," said Pete.

I moved toward him and he stood his ground. He'd try, I'd give him credit for that, he'd try until he was bloody hamburger.

"Hideo!" Mrs. Henderville called sharply. The round brown face peered around the corner as she spoke, and he pattered to her, bowing.

"Call the sheriff's office. Tell them to come here at once."

I grabbed him by the mess jacket and slapped him across the head, and the little cuss tried some judo. Pete came in from behind me and the three of us went sprawling across the floor, knocking over a table. Hideo got the hand chop on the throat —it seemed kind of popular today and it seemed only right that he'd get put out of the ball game with a judo cut—and Pete and I wrestled. He was stronger, bigger, and knew more about it until I got an elbow into his face. Use an elbow like a hammer, and bones and teeth go. After the first one, he took the others limply.

When I stood up Pete was holding his broken face and Hideo was rubbing his throat and trying to swallow air. I was fighting madness, kill madness. My hands were working, clenching, unclenching, and I couldn't breathe enough air to satisfy my blood.

"Goddamn you to hell," I yelled at the Henderville woman, "start talking or I'll tear this kid of yours apart!"

She was a sportswoman; she belonged to those strangers who lived in another dimension from mine. With her son trying to spit out blood and broken teeth, holding his hands to his smashed cheekbone and nose, she made no gesture of sympathy to him. She stood a few feet from Wild and looked at her.

"You're obviously mad or ill or under the influence of dangerous drugs, young woman. For your own sake it would be well if I called for help. Will you see that this thing here doesn't molest me?"

Wild came to me and put her hands on my face. But in the need to destroy that had swept through me I almost struck her as she touched me. Then it was gone, and I was myself again.

"I'm all right now," I gasped.

"Mrs. Henderville, please," said Wild, looking over my shoulder at the cold, gray, remote woman. "We know you lied. We're trying to find out why."

"There was no lie. Mr. Brown was here with my son and myself until nearly four this morning. Our houseboy served us coffee and brandy at intervals until then. I am, of course, prepared to state this under oath."

Hideo scuttled like a crab, and was out of the room. Pete pushed himself up from his knees with one hand, the other still held to his smashed face. He stumbled away.

Wild and Sue Henderville were fighting a wordless conflict of eyes, and neither looked away. "You're lying because of your son," said Wild. "Brown had something on him. Is that right?"

"My son has been injured. You can prevent me from calling for help only by further violence."

She turned and started to walk away. Wild grabbed her, spun her around. "It's no good, do you understand? It's no good. You can't win. Start telling the truth or you'll get your violence!"

Sue Henderville tried to break away.

"I'm fighting for my man. I'll rip the truth out of you if I have to!" This was Red Kearny's daughter, not something elegant from a Connecticut finishing school.

"It's the truth!" Sue Henderville's voice was high and frightened.

Wild slapped her hard.

"You're lying. What's Brown got on you?" She stopped suddenly.

Hideo came back into the room, holding a big, black Army .45, pointing it at me. He was using both hands.

"I kill him," he squeaked, and the room was a blast of sound. There was a clattering tinkle of falling glass somewhere.

"Come on, Wild," I shouted, grabbing her arm and pulling her toward the open panel.

We got to the opening and there was another blast. Some of

the glass ten feet from us shattered and fell.

Down the steps and there was a third one. God only knows where that slug hit.

We were in the MG and Wild gunned it up to sixty in fifteen seconds, with the rear wheels sliding on the first curve.

"The sheriff will be here in a couple of minutes. We've got to get away!" I said loudly.

"I tried, Jim, I tried," she said.

I bent over quickly and kissed her. We wouldn't have much time together now, and these few seconds in the car, high above the moonlit Pacific with the pine scent rich in the air, were unbelievably precious.

We had so little time, we had found each other so quickly and in such violence.

"All the strength is in that woman. I know her kind. She'll die before she lets the world look down on her or pity her." Wild turned the car up a steep, hill-circling road.

"Who is your father's best friend in New York? Better if it's a lawyer."

"Max Schoenberg. Smart, honest, and a good friend."

"We'll find a phone and you call him collect. Our only chance now is to have friends."

"Right, Jim. I'll find a phone."

"The sheriff will try to block off the Peninsula. They'll probably catch us within minutes. If you can call, give Schoenberg the whole story, step by step. Right up to the Jap shooting that big forty-five."

"If they catch us before I can call, then what?"

"We'll try our best to keep from getting caught. If they do—"

"If they do it will be the both of us together," she said. "They can't beat a team that keeps fighting, Jim."

"We're going to have to dump the car. They have the license. If from nowhere else, they have it right in the Carmel police accident file for Saturday." I was trying to think against the police now, the way an officer leading a patrol in enemy country has to think against the enemy. We needed those minutes to get a call to Max Schoenberg, to get our story—the true story—to somebody with strength.

"I know the Forest pretty well, Jim. We're going to come out above the Presidio, where the Army Language School is. We'll park among all the cars in the lot there, and we can walk down through the Presidio to Fishermen's Wharf. We can go into a restaurant and put in our call."

Suddenly the Forest was behind us, and Wild swung through the gate and down a broad, straight residential street. A few blocks down she turned to the right on another wide avenue. In the distance now we could hear sirens screaming through the night.

The Presidio is a small Army post set on a hill above Monterey Bay. Wild drove the MG down the main road and took us into a big parking lot for the military students.

A minute later we were walking down a steep, curving road toward the lights of Fishermen's Wharf.

"When you put in the collect call to Schoenberg, who will you say is calling?"

"Why, Wild Kearny, of course. Oh, I see. The operator would recognize the name, maybe."

"If she reads the Sunday papers she will."

"I'll say Miss Kearny—that should get by. Do you have any money, Jim?"

"About a nickel."

"I stopped being hungry back there in the cottage, but I think we both need a drink. A double shot, straight."

We walked out of the shadows of the Presidio into the lights of a big service station. A block away was the Wharf and a clock in the station showed nine-forty-five. It was about the best part of Sunday evening in a warm, fine January on the Monterey Peninsula. For a moment I forgot that I had killed a man tonight, that I had maimed another man's face, that we were hunted as psychotic killers by the police.

Chapter Eighteen

The wharf is a jumble of sea-food cafes, bars, and a little theatre, and scattered among them are good, honest fishermen's shops that sell the heavy tackle of ocean fishing. It's a few hundred feet long, as wide as a street, and it smells the way it should.

Wild and I walked through the wandering groups of winter tourists and I tried to pretend we were what we were not until the lights in front of the Wharf Players showed me the blood on my coat sleeve from Pete Barrow's face.

"It hasn't been a night of very good surprises for you, has it, Jim?"

I thought Wild had seen the blood. "No. There've been a lot of surprises, and only one of them was good—you."

"I've got a nice little one. Come with me."

We went into a little hole-in-the-wall bar. An elderly Portuguese lady was sewing on something colorful and lovely behind the bar. When she saw Wild she stood up smiling, waving her arms, welcoming her in Portuguese.

"This is my good friend," Wild said to me, "and she doesn't speak English very well. Not well enough to hear news broadcasts or read papers. Best of all, I often come in here with a crowd and pay her at the end of the week."

The lady was smiling at me and she looked as if she liked me. Wild sat down on a high stool.

"What do you want, Jim?"

"A double Scotch straight. Water in a glass, please."

Wild pointed to the bottle, indicated a straight double.

The drink washed away a lot of strain I hadn't known I had. Things shifted into perspective. It was going to take explaining to get me out of the shadow of that thin body with the broken neck. It was going to take strength to crack the steel will of Sue Barrow Henderville and make her tell the truth.

The clock behind the bar pointed to two minutes after ten. I reached toward the corner and turned on the radio. There was music.

"I'm going in back and phone," said Wild. She slid from the stool and walked behind the bar. She pointed to the cash register and made a writing motion. The lady smiled and nodded, as if paying for drinks were not very important at all.

Wild and I looked at each other before she stepped through the curtain to the room in back. It was a look between a man and a woman who knew each other and liked what they knew.

I sat on the stool and stared at my empty glass. The lady made filling motions but I shook my head. The double had done the trick. I knew where I was in the world, what I had to do.

A fat man in a gaudy shirt came into the little bar from the Wharf. The lady looked at him with a mixture of dislike and respect. He had a big, red face, with a halo of curly white hair around his bald head. His bare forearms were thick and strong, covered with tight-curled black hair. There was a nest of mixed white and black hairs like springs rising up from the open shirt.

He put a hand on my arm and smiled. He was smoking a thick black cigar that he had to take away from his mouth before he could smile. I remembered him from somewhere.

"I'm your friend," he said. "I know who you are. When the girl comes back I want to talk to you."

"Who are you?" Even as I asked, I knew. Carmel, Saturday night, with Brown.

He kept smiling, the cigar close to my face, his arm on mine. He had an immense stomach, but behind the fat was a fisherman's muscle.

"I told you. I'm your friend." He laughed.

It was the damnedest laugh, almost like a baby's laugh.

"Where do you know me from?" This big cupid with the halo of white hair and the net-hauling muscles didn't bother me much. Wild was in the next room talking to Max Schoenberg. It was one o'clock in New York, he'd be home, and she had said that he was tough, smart, and a good friend. That was what we needed.

"I don't know you real well, but we have some good friends." He laughed again.

The music on the radio stopped.

"We bring you a news bulletin. James Work, escaped killer of a wealthy society girl in Carmel last night, has apparently added another victim. A Carmel resident known as Buddy

Brown was found by police tonight in his cottage dead from a broken neck. Fingerprints found in the cottage indicate that James Work may be the killer.

"Work had tried to implicate Brown in the murder of the girl and made his escape after witnesses offered an alibi for Brown. Police say—"

The fat man turned off the radio.

"Broken neck. You're real strong for a kid your size." The thick fingers hooked into my arm like gaffs and the hard eyes were dead cold and small. "Why'd you kill the punk, huh? Talk. The old lady doesn't understand."

Wild came through the curtain. She saw the fat man and stopped. They knew each other, I could see that.

"Hello, Joe," she said.

"Hello, princess. I was just talking to your boy friend. Your new boy friend, I mean. Ha-ha."

"It's fine, Jim. I talked to him. He's flying out on the early-morning plane. He says if we want to we can give ourselves up, but he'd rather be here when we do it. He's wiring five hundred dollars tonight to me as Mary Cash, waving identification. He says not to worry about anything. He'll be here tomorrow afternoon, late."

She was trying to tell me everything while she had the chance.

"This is Joe Sandodera, Jim. I met him several times in the last few days with Buddy. He and Buddy had a deal."

The fingers stayed deep in the flesh of my forearm. I had to take it. I couldn't risk trouble.

"You didn't have to introduce us, princess. This boy and I got good friends together. You want to come along, huh?" He chuckled around the cigar.

I got off the stool. The Portuguese lady looked worried and Sandodera spoke to her.

"Her old man's the bartender. The law says a woman can't serve drinks, but she don't know about that law. They don't have it in the old country. Ha-ha. Let's go." The last two words were flat; he meant them.

Wild walked from behind the bar. She looked at me and I shrugged.

"Funny thing," said Sandodera. "I wouldn't have known my

pal here if I hadn't seen you sitting in this joint. Right away I put two and two together—this is the fellow I want to meet and everything's george. Funny, huh? All the cops looking for you, and who finds you? Me." This time he really knocked himself out laughing. He ended up coughing.

"Want to go with this clown?" I asked Wild.

"All I know about him is bad," she said.

"Ha-ha." Then the fingers really went to work on my arm. This man was a giant of muscle.

"Schoenberg says give ourselves up tonight?" It was hard to talk because of the pain, but I was trying to act as if Sandodera were only an annoying barroom drunk. Not easy with his big red face close to mine, his gaff-hook fingers in my arm.

"He says better not until he gets here."

"O.K., clown. We'll go."

"Everything's george, huh?" Nothing seemed to make Sandodera angry. The three of us walked out of the bar into the wind-swept coolness.

He led me with his arm. Wild followed. There were plenty of people around and now that Schoenberg was coming I wasn't worried. If I remembered the rules, he couldn't practice law in California, but he could give a lot of enthusiasm to some local law wheel. To hell with this muscular cupid with the polar-bear hair. I felt great.

"The boat's right below here." Sandodera pointed to a flight of wooden stairs leading down from the Wharf.

"What boat?"

"Go ahead!" He gave me a shove and I fell down half the flight until I caught the railings. Wild was behind me, Sandodera behind her.

I went down to a wooden platform. The boat, a small purse seiner, was bumping the pilings, her rigging banging gently.

"Get in. We're not going anyplace, don't worry."

I helped Wild over the side. The big nets were piled high on the short, broad deck. The cabin and pilothouse were forward, with a small flying bridge above.

Sit down. We can talk private here. Want a drink? I got a couple bottles in the cabin." He motioned to some boxes on the deck. Wild and I sat on them.

No. O.K., so you know I'm Jim Work. Now what?" Well,

kiddo," he said, thumbs in his belt, standing over me, "I didn't know you were in this tough a jam. I didn't know you killed the punk. Why did you do it? Because of this tomato?"

I didn't say anything. A dozen feet above us was the Wharf, all around us were other fishing boats, and apparently we were alone on this one.

"Yeah, that's your business, kiddo. You're like me, like the great Sandodera. If you got to kill 'em, do it with your hands. Crack! Break a back, snap a neck. Take 'em out on the boat far enough, throw 'em to the eels. Ha-ha-ha-ha." He slapped me on the back. "But I wouldn't do it for a tomato. World's full of tomatoes. Sometimes I have three, maybe four of them on this tub, all trying to scratch each other's eyes out."

He lit his cigar, chuckling.

"I'm not from this port, kiddo. I'm from down south. That's what we want to talk about. How much you got for me?"

"How much what?"

"Uncut Japanese number-one white. Like the punk showed me a sample."

"Heroin?"

"Sure, heroin. What the hell did you think I wanted from you?"

"What makes you think we've got friends in common? You mean Brown?"

"Brown?" Sandodera spat. "Who calls that punk a friend?" He turned to Wild.

"Excuse me, princess. I forgot about you."

"Who do you mean?"

"The kid on the General Hanford. Who else? Ha-ha."

I didn't say anything. The fat man was waiting. Then his hand slapped my face gently.

"There was maybe fifteen or twenty thousand bucks wholesale of uncut Japanese ichiban on the General Hanford. The kid brought it over, gave it to you. You gave Brown one box. I want the others. You can't peddle the stuff, you're so goddamn hot now you're blistering that box under you. I'll make a deal. Come up."

"Why do you figure me in this?"

"I called my finger at Fort Mason after I heard the news about the box they picked up in your car. My finger says you came in on the Hanford. The law finds one box in your car. Brown, the punk, said he had a box off the Hanford and he eave me a sample. Damn good Japanese heroin. That adds up easy. You've got two, maybe three boxes left. Brown said no other buyers but me were here or knew about the stuff. I want all of it, kiddo—and I'll deal good with you."

The festering trail of Buddy Brown. Wherever he went there was this.

"Understand, kiddo, you don't have any choice. You can't make a better deal because I'm the combination's man. I'm the buyer for the combination. I'll take care of you and the princess. She says some guy is flying here, not to get picked up until he's arrived. O.K. make yourself at home on the tub."

He spat out a piece of cigar. "Five grand a box. I'm not chiseling because you're hot. Five G cold for each box. Tell me where they are, I send a punk to pick 'em up. When I get 'em and they check out, you get the loot. O.K.? Everything george, ha-ha."

I was trying to balance the play in my mind. Sandodera was deadly dangerous, a child would know that. Immensely strong, cruel, selfish. Being with him was being in danger.

But it might not be easy to prove my innocence on Brown's box of heroin. The very closeness that Wild and I had found together was against us. I'd come from the port of Yokohama on the Military Sea Transport Service General Hanford. The heroin had been smuggled in on that ship. It had been found in my car.

A few other soldiers had tried the gamble—smuggling in a small fortune in Japanese narcotics, as easy to buy in the black market of the Shimbashi in Tokyo as liquor or women. I couldn't prove that I hadn't been one of them. They wouldn't believe Wild because she was in love with me. They knew that Wild and I had been lovers on the night of Pen Brooks' death.

Schoenberg might find ways of getting the truth out of Mrs. Henderville and Pete Barrow. He might convince a jury that I had killed Buddy Brown in self-defense. But heroin brought over on the ship that I had been on, heroin found in my car ...

"Howsabout it, kiddo?"

"What do I know about you?" I asked.

He slapped me on the back and laughed, holding his belly. "You're no punk, hey, kiddo, ha-ha!"

I spoke to Wild. "You know the picture. It's the gimmick about the car. This one might be the right one—but there's a risk. I'm going to go along for two reasons, tonight and the payoff. Understand?"

It was double talk. I had to hope she understood. Sandodera's eyes were closed to black, glittering lines.

"Brown was afraid of you," Wild said to him.

"Sure he was afraid of me," Sandodera growled. "He thought he was tough, but Sandodera was what the punk was praying to be. I kill with my hands, like you do, kiddo, and when I see a tomato I want—" He laughed and threw his cigar into the water. He poked me with a spike of a finger. "You knew the punk, you don't know me good yet. I'll tell you a story. You know who Sandodera is? Sandodera is the man from the combination.

"You know who your friend was? Nothing! A schnook! But a schnook with a cute racket. He'd find a young broad —just the right one—with a guy overseas. Then he'd sell the girl on a big story about how she could have minks and diamonds and a fancy car. All she had to do was get the boy overseas to smuggle a little Japanese heroin back to the States. The punk would tell the girl he'd find a place for them to raise the dough, and how to send it to Tokyo. When the kids came back he'd have the buyer with the big money ready. For a schnook it was a good scheme. All the C.I.D. could ever trace was the broads—if they traced anything."

He reached over and grabbed my arm, the spike fingers digging under the muscle. "I been waiting on this lousy tub for two days more than I figured. For a week the punk played around, giving me a sample, talking big, trying to up the price. He thought he could get in with the big boys through Joe, ha-ha-ha. I been walking the Wharf all evening waiting for him, and he can't show because you busted his neck. Ha-ha-ha. Good joke, but no more jokes. Where's the rest of the stuff?"

"How do you figure me in this?"

The fingers tightened.

"The combination ain't stupid, kiddo. We watched the punk operate. He got three girls to raise six grand from an L.A. shylock with the dough going to their guys in Tokyo. We traced that. Six G in Tokyo, American green money, buys twenty G's worth of heroin, at wholesale prices delivered here. Brown was going to pay the shylock eight and diddle the kids out of their share. We knew that.

"We know that four packages went on the Hanford. We contacted the three guys as soon as the Army brought them off the ship and to the separation center. They were clean. The stuff had been passed to another soldier, who was going to take it to the dealer, and the dealer was Brown. We couldn't find who was the other soldier, the guy who brought the stuff to Brown.

"Now I know who he is. You. What are you trying to do, kiddo? Figure some cute angle of your own? For you there ain't any cute angles, ha-ha."

Now I know enough of the story for the Army's C.I.D. and the Federal Narcotics Bureau to trace the whole lousy mess. Three soldiers who had been in Tokyo, who had wives or girls in Los Angeles, who came in on the Hanford. Out of the two thousand men on the ship, only a hundred, maybe, would fill those particulars. Out of those hundred, three were the greedy, stupid, dirty ones. They'd find them, thanks to the Los Angeles and Buddy Brown lead. And I would give them Sandodera.

For a man in a bad jam, I felt good. I'd never feel guilt for having killed a rat like Brown. The only girl I wanted was my girl now. I knew I could fight my way out of the jam.

I was through with Sandodera now.

"Get your crumby paw off my neck," I said.

"You tough kiddo?"

"Get back on the Wharf, Wild," I said.

Sandodera put out a big arm to stop her. "I wasn't going to do this until after a while," he growled, and he grabbed her by the throat, his other hand still in my shoulder. He gave me a shove and, holding Wild by the throat he pushed her into the open cabin hatch. I was on his back and he turned, grabbing me with both arms like a bear.

Holding me in the bear squeeze, he threw me into the cabin. I was up fast but he was standing there ready for me. Wild was crouched behind me and there was no room for movement. I hit him three times. It was like hitting a bull.

I felt his arms go around me again in the rib-breaking, lung-smashing bear squeeze. I tried to fight him and Wild hit him with something that tore his forehead.

The big red face, the white halo of hair, the cold eyes were in front of my eyes and the thick arms were tightening on me. Blood was trickling down his face and Wild hit him again but the arms kept tightening.

She stuck her thumb in his eye and the arms dropped but he threw a left into my belly like a sledgehammer and I went down. He knocked Wild on top of me and stood above us, one hand to his bleeding eye.

He was crying, his mouth twisted down like a bawling baby's and he was cursing us in sobs, cursing in some strange language.

Then he pulled Wild up by her hair and slapped her with his other hand, terrible slaps with his thick hand and his powerful muscles.

I kicked him from the floor and he was hurt. He dropped Wild and came for me. She fell against the cabin bulkhead. I got my heel into his face as he came down, pushing him back. I was still on the cabin deck and he was on me again, his hand grabbing for my foot as I tried to kick. He got my throat, pulled me from the deck, and hit me. That was it. I was still conscious, but my body control was gone. The sledge hammer got me on the side of my head and I was out.

I came back because of shock and pain. I had fallen into some kind of big box. I looked up at the cabin's beams. My knees were doubled up and the box wasn't wide enough for my shoulders.

I saw Wild's face above the box for a moment as I started to struggle to get out of it and then her face came down to me and the weight of her body was on top of me.

"Have fun, you," yelled Sandodera. Wild was pushing on my chest, trying to get up from me. "Have lots of fun. It's your last chance, kiddo. After a little bit I make you tell me where the stuff is, then I work this tomato, and then you meet some eels, a long way down." He closed the lid on the box and fastened it.

Wild screamed, the sound tearing into my ears. Maybe the tourists on the Wharf could hear her, or the fishermen on the nearby boats.

We could hear music, suddenly loud. Sandodera had turned on a radio, and then both the radio and Wild's screams sounded dull and leaden. He had thrown something, maybe a blanket, over the box.

"My fault," I said. It was already hard to talk.

"Couldn't help it," said Wild.

"Suffocate," I mumbled. It was hot and thick even after a few seconds.

"Little air from sides, not much. Don't talk."

I tried to move, but any movement I made pushed Wild against the sides or the top of the box.

"Love you." I knew it might be one of the last things I would ever say.

"Love you, Jim. We've had it kind of rough." And I knew she was smiling.

We didn't try to talk after that.

We lost consciousness slowly, as if our minds were running out, drop by drop.

Chapter Nineteen

Light above me and coolness. No weight on me. Terrible pain beginning to explode in my bones. This was consciousness.

He dragged me, sodden and limp, up and out of the box. Wild was on the deck, clawing at it with her hands. I couldn't stand erect either, and I fell, my body a sack poked by millions of blazing hot needles.

Like Wild, I gasped in great lungfuls of cool air. Cool, thin air with oxygen. I began to rub myself, tearing the wet, crushed clothes from my chest, rubbing my arms and legs. I had killed Buddy Brown. I was going to kill Joe Sandodera, slowly. Somehow I'd live to do that.

He was there in the little cabin, looking at us. His eye was blood-red and swollen, and there was a crust of blood on his forehead.

"Pretty soon my crew will be back. Tell me where the stuff is. Otherwise I throw you back in the box and take you to sea. You want to go back in the box, huh?"

This was the first time in these two days that I was afraid. I was more afraid of that box than I would be of death. I had to fight myself to keep from begging him, praying to him, not to put me back into the box.

"My crew are my boys. They'd watch me cut you both up into shark bait and laugh. I got something pretty nice for them here after I get done with her. What I mean is you'd better tell me where the stuff is goddamn fast."

I got up, holding to a bulkhead, tottering on my rubber, pain-filled legs.

"I'll tell you," I said.

"Where?"

That was a damn good question.

"In an icebox." I was trying to whip my sick mind into action, inventing a story.

"What icebox? Where?"

"In a little bar on Alvarado. The bartender thinks it's just a package. He's holding it for me." Now I knew what my mind had been trying to figure out through the fog of pain. I had wished for an answer, and my mind had followed my wish. It had brought out of the blood mist the words "In an icebox." An icebox that held a secret a bartender had told me a week ago.

"Will he give the box to me?"

"Only to me personally." I had to gamble on that icebox. It had an answer for me.

"It's twelve. The goddamn bars won't be open only two more hours."

"I'll take you there." If the icebox still held the same secret as last week...

His good eye was a narrow slit. "You got cute tricks, kiddo?"

"The only trick is if the cops don't spot me."

He looked at my torn shirt. "I'll give you a fisherman's shirt and jacket and cap. I want that stuff."

"How about her?"

"I tie her up good. My boys won't bother her until they know I'm finished."

Desperately I hoped that Wild wouldn't scream now, that Sandodera and I could get to the bar without being spotted by the police.

He rolled Wild over, tied her wrists behind her with a length of cord. He tied her slim ankles. "You won't scream, maybe, because of the cops, but I take no chances." He took tape from the wall cabinet and taped her mouth.

"Rest easy, kiddo," he said to her. "You have a good time after a while." He looked at me, went to a locker, and threw me some clothes. I put them on.

"You being too goddamn good, kiddo. What's the trick?"

"No trick. I'm whipped."

"Maybe. Maybe. Come on."

We went out of the cabin, up the stairway to the wharf.

"If a cop spots you, you got nothing to do with me, understand, kiddo?"

"Yeah. If a cop spots me I never heard of you."

We walked the length of the Wharf, quiet now, with only two or three of its cafes still open.

A block, going by the old custom house, an ageless adobe, and then into the Sunday-night brawl of Alvarado, where the soldiers from Fort Ord were trying to drown the reality of tomorrow's reveille in tonight's beer.

"It's this one," I said to Sandodera as we reached the middle of the block. An M.P. patrol sedan had passed us but we hadn't seen any police.

"O.K."

"You'll have to come up with the money for a couple of beers."

"O.K." He was wary, suspicious.

We went in. It was a small place, one girl, four or five soldiers at the bar. I had stopped in there several times in the last three weeks; the bartender remembered me and said, "Hiya." This was the one who had shown me the secret.

"Two beers," I said, sitting on a stool well beyond the soldiers. Sandodera sat next to me and threw a dollar on the bar.

"I'll get the stuff," I said. I walked to the end of the bar, where there was a sign, "Men." The bartender paid no attention to me. I stepped behind the bar, slid the cover from the icebox, and took out the .45 I knew he kept there.

Joe was standing about ten feet from me.

I'm not a killer. I blew his right knee to pieces. I'm a good shot with an Army .45. He spun around and fell over.

No matter what else happened, he wouldn't have a right leg any more. I figured maybe we were even. Now I would try to send him to prison.

I threw the gun on the floor and put my hands high. Everybody was yelling and screaming. I just kept my hands high. When the cops came I didn't want them to get worried about what I might do.

Good mind. I told my mind I wanted to kill Sandodera and it searched until it found the memory of this bartender showing me his gun and where he kept it in case of a holdup.

They grabbed me now, the bartender and the soldiers.

The cops got there and they slipped cuffs on me, pushed the crowd away. An ambulance was rolling up in front of the place for Sandodera. He was moaning.

"I'm Jim Work," I told the police. "Wild Kearny is in the cabin of a boat at the end of Fishermen's Wharf, bound and gagged. Better hurry."

They hustled me into the back of a squad car and sirened

down the block and out to the end of the wharf.

"Quite a weekend for you, Work," said the policeman next to me in the back of the car. "Kill a girl. Kill a guy. Escape from jail. Almost beat a man to death in front of his mother. Shoot another man."

"It's been quite a week end," I agreed.

"What a character!"

The car squealed to a stop. They hurried down to the boat and they were carrying Wild up the stairs just as the two members of Sandodera's crew arrived. They arrested them on general principles.

Wild saw me and smiled. They were going to take her to the hospital and that's where I wanted her to be.

They took me back to the jail and put me in a cell all by myself. I didn't try to tell them anything. Max Schoenberg was coming.

"Hi, pardner! Mighty sorry to see you back." It was Billy Dooley in the other cell, calling to me.

"You O.K., Billy?"

"Why, sure. I've got social security, if nothing else. But what in the name of jumping frogs have you been doing? Killing people?"

"Killing. Beating. Shooting. I broke one dope pedler's neck and shot another one. Billy—"

"Yeah, pardner?"

"What are you being held for now?" My mind was working real fine tonight.

"Now, that's a funny question, pardner. You know what they're holding me for? Vagrancy. Me, Dooley the Fantastic, being held for vagrancy. Of course, it ain't the first time."

"Not for borrowing that Jaguar?"

"The mark I borrowed it from wouldn't press charges.

"Where did you borrow it?"

"Off the driveaway of some little place in Carmel."

"When?"

"About two o'clock in the morning."

"What was the man's name who owned the Jag?"

"Not sure I remember, pardner. The cop mentioned it, though. Barrow, I think."

It was all pretty obvious now.

Chapter Twenty

When Wild and I had left the Zoo, Pete had been there drinking. Pen, contemptuous of the man who had wanted to marry her, had been in the bedroom.

Billy Dooley had stolen the Jaguar sometime after two o'clock Sunday morning. Pete was still there.

Pete and his mother were willing to alibi Buddy.

Buddy Brown had come to the Zoo when Pete had just stabbed Pen Brooks. Buddy Brown saw a golden future. Get Pete out first, get away himself, blackmail Pete Barrow for the rest of his life.

When we came, finding him over the dying girl, Buddy wanted Pen to die. Alive, she was worthless to him. Dead, she was worth a fortune in blackmail. That was why he had tried to stop Wild from phoning the doctor.

He knew the house would be searched, knew that his place might be searched. He put the package of heroin in my car, walked to a cab stand, and took a cab to the Pebble Beach home of Pete and his mother. They kept him for the night, arranged an alibi.

What kept Pete from taking the easy road—blaming Buddy? It would have been one man's word against another's. There had to be a reason. I'd think about that one.

I went to sleep thinking about it.

Next morning they arraigned me in front of a judge who looked at me with sad wisdom. I pleaded not guilty to a long list of charges.

They took me upstairs and I gave them a long, completely truthful statement. I didn't tell them about Billy Dooley and the stolen Jaguar. That would be for Max Schoenberg later.

Naturally, my statement didn't sound so completely truthful to the police and the district attorney. They questioned me for a long time about it and then gave up for the day.

"I want to talk to Dooley," I said to the jailer as they were getting my stuff out of the locker before they took me to the county jail in Salinas.

"Dooley ain't here."

This was a punch below the belt. Dooley was a star witness against Barrow, and I knew that Billy would be hard to find once he left Monterey.

"Dooley got ten days for vagrancy and six months suspended for breaking jail. The judge liked the kid and he figured that you were the hardened criminal that made him go with you after you closed the door on Stevie. Dooley's out on the truck, helping keep the city clean. For the next ten days."

It was a habitable cell in the Salinas jail and I had a good long nap until Max Schoenberg arrived. The first thing he said was that Wild was doing fine.

Max Schoenberg was a wide-shouldered, rangy man with all the patience in the world. His hair was snow-white. The local man with him was quiet and friendly. He wanted to hear everything I could tell him.

Schoenberg thought about the Barrow angle for a long time.

"You're right," he said, "there must be some pretty strong evidence against Barrow somewhere or he'd have accused Brown instead of giving in to his blackmail. A picture, maybe. Young people like Wild and her friend would be likely to have a flash camera around. It's my bet that this Brown came in, saw Barrow bending over the girl, and just picked up the camera and shot the picture. From what you say, Pete would be no physical match for him, and Brown had the evidence against Pete cold in the camera. He probably left the camera there at the house when he ran out.

The quiet, friendly local attorney seemed impressed with the idea.

They left, I slept some more, and after supper Max came back. He was smiling. They took us to a conference room and he showed me a photo print. It was a good clear flash picture of Pete Barrow still holding the scissors and bending over Pen.

"Before we opened the camera we had the Carmel police take Brown's fingerprints off the shutter release, the flash bulb, and the focusing knob. I talked to Wild at the hospital —she's doing wonderfully—and she said that Brown liked to fool with the camera. It was on the bookshelf next to the bedroom door. This Brown seems to have been a fast thinker."

"Now what happens?" I asked.

"The Monterey sheriff has arrested the Barrow boy. When he saw the picture he broke down."

"How many things does that leave them holding me for now?"

He smiled. "Not so many. Sandodera has a long string of narcotics arrests. The police found about two pounds of crude opium in his boat, so he'll be on his way on a charge of possession, along with his crew. I hope he gets a long trip.

"I'm guessing that the coroner's jury is going to find that Buddy Brown met his death by misadventure. Miss Kearny's story corroborates yours, and the knife, again with Brown's fingerprints, was found near his body. In any case, it's clear self-defense, but the coroner's jury can save everybody a lot of time and money. That's the feeling I get from the county people.

"Neither the Barrow boy nor his mother intends to press charges on the assault. Nobody's angry about your shooting Sandodera except the bar owner, and I gave him a hundred dollars. He's happy."

"What are they holding me for, then?"

He laughed. "Nothing."

I got up from the chair. "You mean I'm free?"

"For a man who was arraigned for murder on two counts, narcotics possession, jail break, assault, and a few minor things, you've got yourself clear in world record time—about nine hours since you were in court.

"We'll go downstairs and get your things. My associate —your actual attorney—is downstairs with a writ from the judge. I'll drive you to the hospital to see Wild. She's expecting you."

"There's one thing," I said.

"Oh?"

"The legal fees and costs. That hundred dollars, your trip, the local lawyer..." Max Schoenberg smiled again.

"You worried about paying?"

I nodded.

"You've got a friend named Broadway Red Kearny. A real friend. Stop worrying."

"What's going to happen to him?"

"I know the story," the white-haired, vigorous Schoenberg said. "Kearny is straight. His taxes are paid. The Eastern combination played politics with a little man in the Internal Revenue office and the Treasury knows already—today, Monday—that they got off on a bad steer. Your friend is O.K..”

“One thing more,” I said. “There's still a lot of Japanese heroin loose somewhere.”

He nodded. “I phoned your story to the Narcotics office in San Francisco. They'd been watching Brown and they picked up his contact in a hotel there last night. He'd mailed the rest of the stuff to Brown in Carmel. They found it in the Carmel post office.”

The friendly, quiet man was waiting for us. The officers gave me my things and we left Salinas in the Monterey attorney's car.

“Poor kid,” said Schoenberg.

“Who?”

“Barrow. Half drunk, angry, and the girl tormenting him. And then, before he quite realized what had happened, there was a bright flash and he turned to see this Brown there with a camera. He left the place with Brown hurrying him, only to find his car gone. He says he walked for an hour before he took a cab home. Brown was there, and his mother. Brown had told her everything except that there was a picture. He was pretty battered from the fight, Barrow says, and he had some vague idea of saying that you and Wild had stabbed Pen.

“In the morning the police brought the Jaguar back—that is, they had it at the station and Pete went there to get it after they phoned. He found out that you were being held for the stabbing, he phoned home, and the deal was set.

“This boy Dooley didn't know the address where he'd stolen the car, the Carmel police didn't make any connection. Naturally Pete didn't press charges.”

We were passing the green and white buildings of Fort Ord.

“Brown's number was up anyway. The Narcotics people knew about his smuggling racket, but they didn't know that Sandodera was in town or that he had a boat. Nailing him has made you kind of popular.”

I thought of the terrible box, of the slug shattering the fat man's knee, of the fact that I wasn't a killer.

They took me to the hospital and I saw my girl.

Chapter Twenty-One

We drove out to the airport in my Ford. It was a beautiful February day on the Monterey Peninsula.

At the airport cafe we talked about a lot of things. College, mostly. We didn't have any classes together but we sort of shared each other's classes. Wild liked the school and it made it mean a lot more to both of us to be there together. So we had coffee and talked. It was wonderful.

When the plane stopped at the end of the runway we watched them roll up the stair and open the door. The first man out was Broadway Red Kearny.

Big man with the warmest blue eyes I've ever seen. He shook hands with me.

"Is this the man, Wild?"

"This is the man," she said.

CPSIA information can be obtained
at www.ICGtesting.com
Printed in the USA
FSOW02n1119061016
25818FS